HOLLOW MOUNTAIN

BY THE SAME AUTHOR

Shadow of the Rock
Sign of the Cross

HOLLOW MOUNTAIN

THOMAS MOGFORD

BLOOMSBURY
LONDON · NEW DELHI · NEW YORK · SYDNEY

First published in Great Britain 2014

Copyright © 2014 by Thomas Mogford
Map by ML Design

Bloomsbury Publishing Plc
50 Bedford Square
London
WC1B 3DP

www.bloomsbury.com

Bloomsbury is a trademark of Bloomsbury Publishing Plc

Bloomsbury Publishing, London, New Delhi, New York and Sydney

A CIP catalogue record for this book is available from the British Library

ISBN 978 1 4088 4658 2

10 9 8 7 6 5 4 3 2 1

Typeset by Hewer Text UK Ltd, Edinburgh
Printed and bound in Great Britain by CPI Group (UK) Ltd, Croydon CR0 4YY

For Ali Mogford

Heaven smiles, and faiths and empires gleam,
Like wrecks of a dissolving dream.
Percy Bysshe Shelley, *Hellas*

PROLOGUE

The late-morning sun beats down on the child's blonde head as she stares out from the Rock. Fourteen hundred feet below lies the Strait of Gibraltar, tankers and liners scarring its gleaming surface. Mountains break the haze on the far side of the water – Africa? Europe? The girl isn't sure. She remembers her parents arguing when the cruise ship docked, her father insisting that Gibraltar was an island, her mother that it was attached to Spain. In the distance, a queue of glinting Matchbox cars waits to drive away onto dry land. Mama was right, then.

The little girl walks on, scuffed red Mary-Janes kicking up the dust. Shielding the path from the sheer drop down the Rock is a crumbling stone wall, which bulges out into a small, curved enclosure. A group of grey-furred monkeys is huddled inside, grunting and swaying like a single multi-limbed beast.

The girl glances round: her parents are still fussing over the baby, slumped mewling as usual in its carry sling. She looks back. One of the monkeys has escaped the throng and leapt onto the parapet wall. It gives a hiss, exposing dirty yellow fangs.

The tour guide strides over, tanned and weather-beaten, king of his tiny domain. 'Come away from the edge,' he barks, 'and don't feed the apes, it's against the law.'

But the child is pointing into the enclosure, where the noise has died down, the squabble mysteriously resolved. They watch in silence as, one by one, the monkeys jump onto the parapet, before clambering down the limestone crags out of sight. The largest remains behind, thick-necked, squatting, its head lowered.

The guide recognises the pack leader, a powerful matriarch who usually shuns the tourists. Beneath her front legs lies a heavy tubular object. As the monkey raises the trophy to her mouth, the man feels his heartbeat quicken. He pulls off his sunglasses, frowning in disbelief as he registers the dangling white strands, the matted wrist hairs, the scattering of sweetcorn-like globules around a protruding nub of bone.

The monkey edges her lips along the tube, as though playing some primitive instrument. Her mouth recoils from a shining metal band, a man's wedding ring, the tour guide realises. Taking a step backwards, he feels a sudden pressure as the little girl clamps herself to his side, sweat-soaked T-shirt muffling her scream.

The monkey's pink-skinned face stretches into an unsettling facsimile of a smile. Then she grabs the severed human arm and vaults away down the Rock.

PART ONE

Genoa

Chapter One

Spike Sanguinetti sat at the deserted café, half-watching the tour groups gather along the esplanade. The main draw appeared to be the aquarium, a vast rectangular building projecting into the bay. Odd to pay to see captive fish with the Mediterranean lapping at your feet.

He ordered a cappuccino, provoking a snort of disapproval from the waiter – in Genoa, it seemed, no one drank milky coffee after breakfast. He requested a slab of focaccia, just to irk the man further, then turned back to the esplanade, watching the tourist queues lengthen as cocksure youths on Vespas cruised the coast road behind, like sharks circling for prey.

The coffee was slapped down, brown liquid catching in its saucer. Spike took in the logo on the side of the cup – Janus, the Roman god of new beginnings, one face turned to the future, the other to the past. He'd seen countless images of the city's mythical founder since arriving in Genoa last month, emblazoned on flags, boats, gateways, the symbolism like a quiet taunt to a man so unable to contemplate his future; so stubbornly drawn to the past. In the distance, a church bell started to toll. Midday had finally arrived.

Spike ate the last of his focaccia, savouring the sea-salt flakes embedded in its crust, then heard a hollow metallic rattle – security blinds rolling down as the merchants of the Porto Antico closed up shop for lunch. Downing his coffee, he rose reluctantly to his feet and set off along the waterfront.

Just past the aquarium was the Museum of Seafaring, a reminder that the industry which historically had enriched Genoa was also the means for so many of its residents to escape. Spike passed Renzo Piano's futuristic white crane, eyes moving to the happy tourists hoisted in its glass lift, snapping photos of the bay. Turning his back on them, he walked beneath an ugly concrete overpass towards a line of palazzos set back from the harbour.

Narrow passageways knifed between grand, faded facades. He slipped inside one, passing a sweating shopkeeper hurrying back towards the light. The twisting alleys – *caruggi*, they were called – led deep into the medieval rump of the port, the buildings on either side eight stories high, washing lines strung between them, what light there was struggling through an arrow-slit of blue. On the corner of a locked-up florist, Spike saw the street name he'd been looking for: Vico Paganini.

The girls were standing in their usual spot. There was nothing particularly outrageous about their appearance – perhaps the stonewash jeans were a little tight, the leather boots an odd choice for this time of year. What was strange was that they did not seem to be going anywhere.

Hearing Spike's footsteps, both girls turned. One looked Bulgarian – not dark enough: Romanian, maybe – the other North African. The Romanian glanced at the building above, then mustered a smile and made her move. '*Vuoi venir' sopra?*'

'*Ho una domanda . . .*' Spike began, but the girl's blank face suggested an entirely pragmatic command of Italian. 'English?' he tried, and she nodded uneasily.

Moving to one side, Spike reached into his pocket and drew out the photograph. 'I'm looking for this woman. Have you seen her?'

The Romanian's smile died, and suddenly Spike could see the puffiness around her eyes, the feverish sheen on her forehead. Her friend approached, slim arms folded tightly across her tank top, and they both stared down at the picture. A scraping came from above: Spike looked up and saw a familiar two-faced symbol surmounting the window. *Janus, Genoa . . .*

'Please, mister,' the North African girl said, shaking her head, 'we . . .' She broke off as the door opened and a bullet-headed Genoese strode out – diamond ear-stud, unbuttoned denim shirt suggesting a profound commitment to the gym. The girls were already back at their stations.

'You talk, you pay,' the Genoese snapped. He lurched at Spike, gesturing at the picture in his hand. Crisp, leather-soled footsteps echoed behind as a suited man appeared. The pimp threw a nod at the Romanian, who made an awkward sashay towards the new prospect. Quickly, Spike flipped over the photograph. At the café he'd written four letters on the back: 'MDMA'. As the pimp read them, his stance relaxed. 'Five minute,' he smirked, walking back into the house.

Spike turned again to the North African. 'Her name is Zahra. She comes from Morocco. Like you, maybe?'

The girl glanced nervously over her bare shoulder. A circuit board of white and pink scars crisscrossed the inside of her arm; acne speckled her cheeks, poorly camouflaged by a layer of greasy foundation. Fifteen years old, or sixteen . . . Spike felt the anger he'd packed so diligently away testing its restraints. Forcing it down, he slipped the photo into the girl's slender hand. 'Or Žigon?' he asked gently. 'Have you heard of a man called Žigon?'

A murmur came from behind as a middle-aged couple appeared, two Asians wrestling with a tourist map. They took in the scene, then vanished back the way they had come.

'Z-I-G-O-N?' Spike spelled out.

A bitter smile caught the girl's lips, too old for her face. 'She is pretty.'

'Yes.'

'Pretty ones do not stay in Genoa.' She moved away, perhaps hearing something Spike had not.

'Where do they go, *signorina*?'

'Follow the money,' the girl laughed, spine straightening.

Spike spoke more urgently now – 'I don't understand' – as the Genoese reappeared, tapping at his breast pocket. 'Where?' Spike hissed. He barely caught the girl's reply, a single word so softly spoken it seemed to float out of the alley and away to sea. '*Paradiso . . .*'

Spike turned back to the pimp. 'Changed my mind,' he said, taking out a grimy ten-euro note. 'Sorry to waste your time.' The man plucked at the money between Spike's thumb and forefinger. Spike held onto it for a moment, then released his grip and walked back towards the waterfront.

Chapter Two

Spike flipped out the light. The guest-house window gave onto the north side of Genoa's cathedral, its black-and-white marble lit up like a humbug to tempt the tourists. He lay back on the metal-framed single bed, leather bag packed and tucked beneath, bill already settled.

As soon as he closed his eyes, Zahra's face appeared. It always seemed to start the same way. An autumn afternoon not long after he'd brought her to Gibraltar, a time heightened by the relief they'd both felt at escaping Morocco and its bad memories. Zahra had abandoned her headscarf by then, and her black hair lay in glossy waves on her shoulders. Spike had shown her round the Alameda Gardens, pointing out the bronze sculpture of Molly Bloom, who in the fictional world of *Ulysses* had grown up in Gibraltar. Zahra hadn't heard of Joyce, but she'd liked how Molly had raised her chin defiantly at the Rock, as if challenging its hulking majesty. A few sentences were etched into the plinth beneath the sculpture, which Zahra had read aloud in her low voice, one thumb hooked beneath the waistband of newly purchased jeans: '. . . *and the sea the sea crimson sometimes like fire and the glorious sunsets and the figtrees . . . I was a Flower of the mountain . . . walking down the Alameda on an officers arm . . .*'

They'd caught the cable car up to the Apes' Den. As they climbed higher, Zahra had pressed her face to the window, watching the limestone crags fall away beneath her. Her breath had condensed on the perspex, and they'd seen an image appear in the mist, a child's finger-drawing of a man and a woman encased in a heart. 'You see,' she'd said, 'I can show you things too.' Spike had known what her smile meant, what she'd wanted him to say, but had pretended not to. She'd looked away, face fallen. Spike hadn't realised it at the time, but something had been lost that day. A month later Zahra had left Gibraltar for Malta. And six months after that she'd disappeared.

Sinking further into sleep, Spike found himself back on the Rock, standing alone on the concrete platform, waiting for the cable car to approach. As it hove into view, he saw Zahra sitting inside, staring up at him, panic in her dark eyes. The car gave a judder as it slotted into the docking station, the wire that held it in place springing loose. As Spike leapt forward, trying to force the doors apart, Zahra turned away, staring down at the drop below as the car lurched. 'Take my hand,' he shouted, and she reached up through the gap he'd wedged between the doors. He grabbed her wrist, but the skin felt cold, and when she looked up, he saw that the face no longer belonged to Zahra, but to the young woman he'd identified in a Maltese mortuary – lips blue, hair clotted with blood, murdered baby at her breast.

The cable car fell away, and Spike watched it crash in slow motion down the Rock, leaving her dangling from his hand as he stumbled closer to the edge. She was slipping, and he registered her look of surprise as she felt the onset of weightlessness just before he let her go. Her scream rose, then faded, as she fell . . .

Spike snapped open his eyes, feeling his heart shift as the scream dissolved into laughter, drunken shouts of revelry carrying up from the cathedral square. He ripped back the sheets, body filmed in sweat. More laughter drifted up, killing the last possibility of sleep. Then he flicked the light back on, reached into his bag and took out his map of the Italian Riviera.

Chapter Three

The next morning, Spike sat at the back of a creaking ferry, watching the creamy wake trail behind into the Mediterranean. The Alpine peaks above the coastline were topped with forts, a railway line ruled aggressively into the hillside beneath. The boat had already stopped at three of the fishing villages along the Gulf of Paradise – Nervi, Recco and San Fruttuoso – where Spike had shown Zahra's photograph at various cafés and hotels, arousing the usual mixture of indifference, pity and suspicion. He stared at it now, smoothing it against his palm, still disturbed by last night's dream. He'd rescued the picture from a barman in Tangiers, just hours before meeting Zahra for the first time. Her shiny black hair was drawn back, her expression suggesting she had not volunteered to be photographed. One eye was covered by a loose lock of hair, and the other . . . The dark brown iris, the delicate almond shape, an innocence her glare failed to mask.

He felt his throat thicken as he remembered the last time he'd seen her alive – slamming the door of a hotel room in Malta. He'd let her go, assuming that she would call once she'd calmed down, like she always did. That they could talk it over, start again. But she had vanished. And this time it was his fault.

Zahra had always had a talent for trouble, he thought. When they'd first met in a shanty town in Morocco, he'd had to push her out of the path of a jeep. She'd been asking the wrong questions, demanding answers like she always did. He'd felt compelled to help her, the man who never liked to get involved. He still didn't really understand why. In the end, they'd made it back over the Straits to Gibraltar – but not before people had got hurt.

They'd had a real chance there to make it work, he felt now. She'd charmed his father, and he'd thought he saw her face soften, the wariness ease in her eyes. Spike had screwed that up too, of course, but their reconciliation in Malta a few months later had been all the sweeter for it. They were both a little older, perhaps even ready to commit. Maybe that was why Spike had chosen to pick an argument with her on their last morning together.

Stupid *charavacca*, he cursed to himself as he slipped her photograph carefully back into his wallet. Zahra's disappearance had now been linked to the people-smuggling ring Spike had helped to break in Malta. It had initially seemed to be a local affair – African migrants scraping together the cash to get to Italy. Yet when Spike and the Maltese police had visited a warehouse outside Valletta . . . His stomach knotted as he recalled the scene. Drugged women chained to camp beds, starved, raped. The body of a dead Somali baby stashed in a freezer. That time, it had been Spike who encouraged Zahra to ask questions in the refugee camps where she worked, unwittingly bringing her to the attention of the man behind it. An individual known in criminal circles only as Žigon.

Spike wished he had a face to put to that strange, sibilant name. Žigon was thought to run the largest prostitution and drug racket in the Mediterranean, and was wanted by Interpol and the police forces of several European countries, yet no one knew his real identity, nor even what he looked like. He was believed to be Slovenian, and had last been seen in Genoa. But then the trail ran cold.

Spike turned back to the coastline, seeing terraced fields rising above the vines and olive trees, cypresses jutting into a picture-perfect sky. It was beautiful, he knew, and felt strangely guilty. He rubbed his stubbled cheeks. The beard he'd allowed to grow since arriving in Italy was long enough now not to itch, and to reveal unexpected patches of grey in the black. His nose remained crooked from the beating he'd received in Malta, when he'd first heard Žigon's name mentioned in connection with Zahra's disappearance. How far had his quest advanced since then? He was saved from considering this depressing question further as the ferry slowed, and he pulled himself to his feet.

The village they were now approaching was the most bijou Spike had seen so far. Within a sheltered inlet, a harbour was enclosed on three sides by soft, ochre-hued houses. A yellow clock tower rose above, powder-puffed by palm trees and acacia fronds. The green interlocking knuckles of the Italian Alps concertinaed in the distance.

The ferry hit reverse as it neared the jetty, its route narrowed by sleek rows of yachts. Their prows all faced to sea, as though trying to escape but held by an irresistible force. Money, Spike thought, seeing a diminutive oligarch steer a willowy blonde towards a waterfront table.

'*Portofino, signore e signori,*' came the ferry's announcement. Then, with a hint of reverence in the tone, the more languid repetition, '*Por-to-fin-o.*'

Chapter Four

Spike checked the time. The next ferry along the Gulf of Paradise was in an hour. He'd already visited the restaurants and bars in Portofino's small but perfectly formed *piazzetta*. There was one place left to try, a pastel-pink palace basking high on the hillside which might have been home to some local *principe*, but for the subtle and tasteful signage he'd seen dotted around the town.

Spike turned up a set of smooth terracotta steps. The creepers on the sidewalls were tamed and sculpted, errant suckers nipped off. Aged plant pots exuded a sweet scent of honeysuckle and jasmine, while chirping cicadas blended with the drowsy hum of bumblebees, one of which Spike watched disappear into a bore-hole so perfectly circular it suggested a gardener had been asked to neaten it up with a chisel.

The steps led to a pathway that emerged onto a canopy-shaded terrace. On the level below was a swimming pool, an infinity lip spilling over the harbour where the ferry had docked. Sunloungers lined it, expensively emaciated women eyeing each other competitively as oblivious men in Vilebrequin trunks ogled their smartphones.

The maître d' was restraining a rebellious tablecloth. He straightened up as Spike approached. 'Good afternoon, *signore*.'

Spike heard the church bell in the village fall silent on the twelfth chime. 'Perhaps you can help me. I'm looking for . . .'

'Reception? Please follow me.'

There existed a level of luxury, Spike thought as he looked down at his scruffy espadrilles and faded blue shorts, when haughtiness reverted to good manners. Another garden staircase, then the maître d' signalled a doorway beneath a jutting Juliet balcony. '*Signore*,' he exhaled, disappearing to the level below before Spike could even open his wallet.

As soon as Spike raised a foot to the first step, a doorman materialised between the hanging fronds of wisteria. He was dark and compact with startling cornflower-blue eyes. He held open the door, and Spike caught sight of his nametag as he passed. '*Enrico Sanguinetti*'.

'Good surname,' Spike said.

The doorman gave a puzzled smile as Spike passed him the tip he'd intended for the maître d'.

Reception was small for such a grand hotel. A tanned redhead sat behind the mahogany desk, green eyes expertly outlined with kohl and showcased by a pair of designer horn-rimmed spectacles. It took her about five seconds to size Spike up, then, 'How may I help you, sir?'

'I'm not sure you can,' Spike replied, leaning in conspiratorially. At the concierge's desk, a bearded man glanced over from behind a computer screen.

'I met a girl in town last night,' Spike went on, offering the receptionist an embarrassed smile. 'I think she may be staying here.' He took out Zahra's photograph and placed it on the desk. The edges looked suspiciously dog-eared on the stained hardwood.

The receptionist drum-rolled two long, red fingernails. 'Don't *think* I've seen her. Michele?'

The concierge came over, shook his head almost imperceptibly, then returned to his monitor. A young couple in immaculate tennis whites entered. The receptionist had unhooked their key before they'd even had a chance to ask for it.

'How about a Mr Žigon?' Spike said. 'Has he checked in recently?'

The cat-like eyes flicked upwards. 'I'm afraid we cannot give out information about our guests. I'm sure you understand, *signore*. But if you'd like to see a brochure . . .' She reached below and placed a glossy white wallet on the desk. The stars encircling the words 'Hotel Splendido' were of embossed gold.

Spike tried a charming grin. 'Or a Mr Radovic?' he asked, remembering an alias Žigon was once thought to have used. The receptionist still had a hand on the brochure, ready to return it to the shelf. As she picked it up, one of her blood-red nails snapped on the desk. She raised the fingertip to her mouth, then handed Spike back the photograph, all traces of playfulness gone. 'Good luck finding your lady friend, sir.'

Chapter Five

As soon as Spike stepped outside, the doorman reappeared. 'Sur-name,' he said. '*Vuol dire cognome, no?*'

Spike took out his wallet and handed him a business card. 'Ha!' the doorman exclaimed in delight. 'You are Sanguinetti also. "Somerset J." . . .' he read uncertainly from the business card. 'Barrister-at-law . . . Gibraltar?'

'Gibraltar's full of Genoese . . .' Spike broke off. 'Is English OK? *Se no, parlo un po' di . . .*'

Enrico Sanguinetti tutted. 'English always good.' He glanced back at reception. 'Come, *Sangui mio,*' he said, signalling to the fronds of wisteria through which he had first appeared. To the side of the building lay an alcove. '*Sigaretta?*' he asked, picking up a soft pack of Merits from beneath a plastic chair.

Spike considered the question, then shook his head and sat down.

'So Gibraltar is *infestato* with Sanguinetti,' Enrico said, lighting up. 'When your family go?'

'Late 1700s. A Genoese merchant called Gustavo.'

'*Gustavo Sanguinetti,*' Enrico echoed with rhythmical pleasure.

'He was more of a pirate than a merchant – used to run a cargo ship armed with hidden cannons. He would sail up to foreign boats, offer to trade, then rob them blind and sell the goods in town.'

Enrico laughed, then took off his red-peaked cap and laid it on the metal table in front of him. 'I think I like this Gustavo.'

'Napoleon didn't. He had to flee to Gibraltar when the French arrived.'

'For me, family is . . .' He rubbed the liveried material of his trousers.

'Draper? Tailor?'

'*Sì*. Tailor. Many generation ago.'

'That must be why you look so smart.'

'And why you do not.' Enrico exhaled pensively, perhaps mulling the past glories of Sanguinetti tailors in Genoa. His dark, thinning hair gleamed with oil. He lit a fresh cigarette.

'How are you with faces?' Spike asked, taking out Zahra's photograph. There was no recognition from Enrico beyond a long slow whistle of admiration. '*Tua ragazza?*' he said.

'She's with another man now.'

'Uh-oh.'

'Called Žigon. Or maybe Radovic.'

'Two names?'

'Yes.'

'Not good.'

'No. Apparently he's well-known on the Riviera.'

'I only start here three months. Before I am at Cipriani, you know?'

Spike heard the sudden blast of a ferry's horn. 'Keep the card,' he said, standing. 'Maybe you could call me if you see the girl. Or a man with two names.'

Enrico beckoned him back and took out his mobile. The screen blinked to life. 'Is *my* baby,' he said, pointing at a coffee-skinned toddler with a broad smile. 'Her mamma and me . . .' He gave a sad grimace, revealing nicotine-yellowed teeth. 'When I have money, I go back to Mestre and help with her life.'

'Sounds a noble plan.'

Enrico refused Spike's tip, then stuck out an arm. 'We are family, uh?'

'Family.'

They shook hands warmly, and Spike headed back down to the port.

Chapter Six

Back on the ferry, Spike flicked through a leaflet advertising a 'Most Historical Tour of Christopher Columbus'. Apparently his family had come from the hills above the coast, before moving to Genoa where the young Christopher had learnt to sail. Spike seemed to recall that it was Genoa's refusal to support Columbus's plan to head west which had forced him to seek sponsorship from the Spanish. No qualms about profiting from him now, he thought, screwing up the leaflet and dropping it into the bin.

Standing by the gunwale, he felt his phone vibrate. Number unknown. As always, he debated whether to take the call – five buzzes, six – then hit the green button just in time. 'Yes?'

The silence was of a crackly distant sort. He was about to hang up when he heard her gentle voice. 'Hello, Spike.'

The ferry seemed to list, and he put a hand out to the railing to steady himself. The calloused black metal was hot to the touch.

'It's me, Spike,' the voice continued. 'Zahra.'

Spike moved his hand to his head, fingers twining through his dark hair. 'Zahra?' he repeated dully. 'Are you OK?' He needed to hear her speak again.

'You have to stop looking for me, Spike.' Her voice sounded strange, but maybe he just hadn't remembered it right. What was it she'd just said? *You need to stop looking for me?* Suddenly it felt as though the decking was sinking beneath his feet. He thought he should sit down, then realised he already was. Forcing himself to take a breath, he found some words. 'I know it must be hard for you to talk, Zahra. Just tell me where you . . .'

The crackling stopped, and for a moment Spike thought she'd hung up. 'Hello?' he said, panicking. '*Hello?*'

'There's no one listening, Spike. I can speak freely. I just don't want you to look for me any more.'

He glanced round, hoping that it was all a joke, that she might be there on the other side of the deck, laughing, waiting for him, arms wide. But all he saw was a teenaged girl on the opposite bench, eyeing him curiously. At her feet, a black Italian mountain dog lay panting thirstily at the sea.

'You have to forget about me, Spike,' Zahra said.

The boat lurched again, and Spike fought the nausea creeping from his stomach into his throat. 'What are you *talking* about?'

'Please – just go home.' A pause: 'I've seen what he can do, Spike. If you don't stop looking for me, it won't be you he comes after. It'll be the people close to you. Do you understand?'

'You're saying he'll hurt you if I don't leave you alone?'

Zahra laughed. A strange sound. 'He would never hurt me. Never.'

Spike felt the drumbeat of blood in his ears. He could sense that the next few seconds were vital. That he didn't have much time. 'Please, Zahra. Just tell me where . . .'

The line went dead. Spike scrolled through his call list, hitting dial on 'Unknown Number', once, twice, three times, knowing it was futile. The teenager was frowning at him now, and he realised that he was slumped on the bench seat, brow slicked with sweat, breathing heavily through his nose. His fist was clenched to his chest, and when he unfurled it he saw four crescent-shaped welts where his nails had dug into the skin of his palm.

As he pulled himself up, a memory of the hotel receptionist in Portofino flashed into his mind, her blood-red talon snapping at the mention of Žigon's alias. Then he was on his feet, running across the deck to the ferry's open-sided wheelhouse. '*Quando torniamo a Portofino?*' he shouted in.

The captain plucked a roll-up from his mouth. 'What?' he replied in English.

'When does the ferry go back to Portofino?'

'Is other boat.'

'But when?'

The captain jabbed behind with a thumb, then took a leisurely drag. 'Soon, *signore*. Soon.'

Swearing under his breath, Spike returned to the balustrade. The ferry was closing in on Rapallo, its pace so sluggish it felt as though they were travelling backwards. He clutched at the railings, rocking back and forth, his movements tracked by the wet, melancholy eyes of the mountain dog.

Chapter Seven

A line of white Mercedes cabs was parked above the harbour, drivers slouching against passenger doors. Spike jogged up the steps towards them. 'Portofino,' he called out. 'How much?'

One driver stepped away from his taxi, shaking his head. 'Not possible, *signore*.'

Spike reached for his wallet.

'No road to Portofino,' the driver shouted close to Spike's face, causing him to recoil from his espresso breath. 'Only boat.' He confirmed this with one of the innumerable Italian hand gestures of which Spike was starting to tire. 'Exclusive,' he added proudly.

'How about the train?'

'Only to Santa Margherita. *Es-clu-si-vo!*'

Spike found himself squaring up to the man, rising to the full extent of his six-foot-three frame, then realised the pointlessness of the confrontation and turned back to the harbour. The ferry he'd just disembarked was already en route for the next stopover. In the ticket hut, the timetable showed that the next boat to Portofino didn't leave for another two hours.

There was a café next to the hut. Spike walked to the bar, feeling the amused gaze of the taxi drivers upon him. '*Doppia grappa, per favore,*' he said to the waitress.

Sitting down at a plastic table, he felt the queasiness pool again in his belly. So Zahra was alive. He'd thought about this moment so many times but had never imagined it would be like this. It just didn't make sense ... She'd called him, but only to ask him to leave her alone. She'd told him her abductor was dangerous, yet insisted she was safe. He raised the grappa to his lips. What if she genuinely didn't want to be found? If she was so ashamed of what had happened to her that she never wanted to see him again?

A low rectangular mirror hung behind the bar. For a moment Spike failed to recognise the angry, bearded man in its reflection. He looked away, feeling frustration flare through him as he signalled to the barmaid, who brought over the entire bottle, insisting on full payment before refilling his glass.

His phone was vibrating. He knocked over the grappa as he scrabbled to answer it, sticky clear liquid oozing onto his bag. 'Zahra?'

'Qué?'

His tongue felt clumsy and furred with liqueur. 'Oh,' he said, identifying the voice of his friend, Detective Sergeant Jessica Navarro, 'it's you.'

'Yes,' Jessica replied impatiently, 'it's me. Can you talk? It's important.'

'Not really. Why? What is it?' There was a pause as he wiped his hand on the thigh of his shorts.

'I'm standing outside your Chambers.'

Spike struggled to keep the irritation from his voice. 'And?'

'It's Peter. Peter Galliano.'

'What do you mean?'

'Somebody's hit him, Spike. With a car. A passerby found him covered in blood.'

Spike rose to his feet, picturing the tight Gibraltar backstreet, a St John Ambulance blocking the way, blue lights rotating as they hoisted Peter aboard . . . 'When?' he said.

'About an hour ago.'

'And he's OK?'

Jessica paused. 'From what the paramedics say, it's touch and go.'

The barmaid came over with a cloth, and Spike stepped away to let her clean the table. 'But he'll recover?'

'It's pretty bad, Spike.'

Out in the bay, the Portofino ferry began its approach. 'Well, keep me informed,' Spike said, nodding at the waitress and picking up his bag. From the other end of the line came a swish of uniformed legs as Jessica walked to a quieter place. 'Keep you *informed*?' she hissed. 'This is Peter we're talking about. Peter Galliano. Your business partner. Your friend.'

Spike took a first step down to the jetty. 'I know. But I can't leave Genoa right now.'

'You're joking.'

'I've just heard from Zahra, Jess. She's alive.'

There was an intake of breath before Jessica spoke. He prepared himself for a tone he knew well. 'Spike. Your best friend is probably going to die tonight. And you want to stay in Italy on some wild goose chase which . . .'

Spike could hear Jessica talking, but her words faded into the background as he remembered Zahra's warning: *It won't be you he comes after. It'll be the people close to you.* He interrupted her, feeling adrenalin starting to heighten his fear. 'When did this happen?'

'About an hour ago, I told you.'

He checked the time: three hours since he'd spoken to Zahra. 'Any eyewitnesses?'

'Not yet.'

'CCTV?'

'It's possible. Nothing so far.'

Spike paused. 'Will you do me a favour, Jess?'

'What?'

'Look in on my father.'

'Why?'

'To . . . tell him about Peter's accident. It'd be better coming from you. In person.'

'If you want. But . . .'

'I'll be back as soon as I can.' She was still talking as Spike killed the call and ran back to the taxi rank.

24

'Genoa,' he said to the new driver at the front of the queue. 'Christopher Columbus Airport.'

*

So I go and meet Hernán in one of those fashionable restaurants just off the Plaza Mayor. You know the sort: blending, *as they would put it,* an ultra-modern decor with an historic location. *Fucking shithole, basically. I'm shown to a table by the door, always a sign they value your custom, and some bread is dumped on the cloth, a couple of stiff roundels of baguette. The plate is deliberately asymmetrical, a sort of contorted china rhombus. Beside it lies a ramekin of yellow oil – cut-price Italian crap, no doubt. I tell the waiter to remove both, then start rearranging the cutlery so that my knife and fork are perfectly aligned. Once I'm done, I look up and see Hernán standing there, grinning like a cat. 'Thought you'd like this place,' he says in his peasant Castilian accent. As usual, his presence has an immediate effect on the servant classes, and the waiter wafts back, tray held high in one limp hand. His bleached blond hair is thin and spiky; a steel bolt pierces his right eyebrow. Right ear, right queer, as they used to say in the Force.*

'El caballero me pidió que los quite,' *the waiter lisps.* The gentleman asked me to remove them.

'Bullshit,' *Hernán replies.* 'I adore French bread.'

The waiter replaces the plate and ramekin with a distinct look of triumph. Oily little fag. I consider leaving, but instead peruse the menu as Hernán sates himself on stale baguette. The usual cultural mishmash: the only local dish is marinated octopus. A couple of years ago you'd have had that as a tapa, *no need to order, let alone pay. Oh Madrid – must you cede to this recession as well? Still, I admit as the food arrives, the meat is nicely marinated, tender and sweet. I eat heartily, watching Hernán nibble at a corner of his Wiener schnitzel. These things are sent to test us.*

We preamble: Hernán's fat wife and her fitness club in Villa de Vallecas, his charmless twin children. He asks about me, and patiently listens as I tell him of the books I have recently revisited – the complete works of San Juan de la Cruz, some Calderón de la Barca. Why does a man with a photographic memory need to reread, Hernán asks, and I give him the same reply as always, that familiar delights taste the sweetest of all. He laughs, then pauses, and I know that we are finally getting down to business.

A glance over one shoulder, then a dip into his record bag (a gift from his wife: I don't need to ask) and out comes the photograph, placed equidistant between my knife and fork.

'Impresionante,' I reply. It is impressive . . . He leaves the image in place long enough for me to commit it to memory, then returns it to his bag.

'Who's the buyer?' I ask casually.

'The usual collector.'

'And that's the only piece?'

'There may be others. We'll have to see.'

'When?'

'That's not clear yet. For now, we just need you to watch and wait.'

'Watch and wait?' I repeat in disgust.

But Hernán is onto dessert now, something called a 'bread and butter pudding', a species of brown turd in a caramel nest. His eyes flick to the frayed cotton of my shirt sleeve. 'It's been a while since your last job,' he says, nut-brown eyes glinting with amusement as he scrapes the dish with his spoon. 'Are you sure you're still up to it?'

I stare back, astonished.

'Of course, the other issue is where you have to go.'

'Abroad?'

'In a sense.'

Hernán signals to our waiter friend for the bill.

'Portugal?' I ask as Hernán takes out his money clip. He smiles but shakes his head.

I shoot the waiter a meaningful glance, then follow Hernán outside. As we stand together in the sledgehammer heat of the Plaza Mayor, sunglasses on, Hernán presses a piece of paper into my hand. On it is written one word: 'Gibraltar'.

PART TWO

Gibraltar

Chapter Eight

Spike Sanguinetti sat idle at his desk, distracted by the sounds drifting in from the backstreets of Gibraltar. Empties smashing into a wheelie bin as the Royal Calpe pub prepared for a new day. The distant buzz of a scooter as some foolhardy soul took on the steep alleyways of the Upper Town. The chatter of locals passing the time before the humidity grew too intense and they retreated indoors.

He looked down at the row of grey lever-arch files stacked up on his desk, half-expecting to hear the usual noises filter in from next door – Peter Galliano on the phone, laughing so hard Spike would assume he was catching up with a friend, before a throwaway line revealed he was talking to a client. The plod of his handmade size-thirteens as he made his way across the parquet to the drinks cabinet, followed by the plaintive call, 'Tell me it's noon *somewhere*'. The mock death-rattle as his ancient computer refused yet again to do what it was supposed to.

Taking a breath, Spike forced himself to pull open the first of the files. Peter's caseload comprised the usual mix of paperwork and court appearances – the legal profession in Gibraltar was fused, so both barrister and solicitor work were available. Of the various cases his business partner had been working on, six could be parked for now, as the trial dates weren't scheduled until next year. Of the remaining eight, one stood out, not just in terms of urgency, but because of the money at stake. Neptune Marine, Inc. . . . Spike gazed again through the French windows, wondering where he'd heard that name before. Cacti seedlings were inching between the paving stones of the patio, their progress untroubled in Spike's absence. Peter never had been much of a gardener . . . He shook his head and pushed deeper into the documentation, reams of paper annotated in Peter's cryptic script. Neptune, it emerged, was a marine salvage company which had recently discovered a shipwreck two and a half nautical miles off the coast of Gibraltar. Keen to raise the sunken cargo, the firm had instructed Galliano to lodge an application with Gibraltar's Receiver of Wreck. So far so straightforward, except . . . Why had the receiver passed the application to the courts instead of handling it directly? And how could a cargo of lead be worth . . . Spike reread the figures. Had Peter misplaced a zero? Four *million* pounds? He scanned through the rest of the correspondence for the contact details of the client, one Morton D. Clohessy – CEO. Had to be American. Clohessy's mobile rang to voicemail so Spike left an urgent message.

He turned to the other case files: a conveyance for a Ukrainian tax exile buying a penthouse in Ocean Village; a fire on a boat – the insurance company alleging arson; a father changing his will after a falling-out with his daughter . . . As he familiarised himself with the documents, he stopped, hearing a strange rustling coming from next door. After one more paragraph, he threw down his fountain pen in defeat and walked into Peter Galliano's office.

The room looked as it always did; the only thing missing was Peter. All but virgin law books on the shelves, a terrible watercolour of a villa Peter owned in Corfu askew on the wall, a stuffed and mangy Spanish wildcat peering down from the windowsill. The rustling came again, quiet and slightly alarming. As Spike moved past Peter's desk, his footfall sent a vibration up to the mouse-pad, causing the computer screen to shimmer back to life, frozen on a still from an online casino advert. He turned it off manually, hearing a deep sigh of relief from within.

A week's worth of takeaway wrappers filled the bin. That was a rat he'd heard, probably, claws scratching away. He bent down to pull out the pungent liner, feeling a deadweight at the base. Nose closed to the aroma of stale falafel, he drew out an empty bottle of Wood's Navy Rum. Not Peter's usual tipple: 57 per cent proof, Spike read grimly, aware that his period of extended leave must have put his partner under even more stress than usual.

The noise began again, and Spike realised that it was coming from outside, something sharp and metallic scraping against the brickwork. He returned to the hallway, ready to throw open the doors, when the buzzer rang. His finger hovered over the button. Then he depressed it and allowed whoever it was to enter.

Chapter Nine

The woman and small boy stepped tentatively into the office hallway. The child clutched a dinky car in one hand; turning to the wall, he ran its wheels up and down the faded paintwork. '*Aliska*, Charlie,' the mother hissed in *yanito*, the dialect spoken by native Gibraltarians, 'not indoors.' She lifted her eyes slowly to Spike's, her smooth white neck emanating a scent of overblown roses.

'How can I help you?' Spike said, self-consciously uncrossing his arms.

'I'm here to see . . .' The woman hesitated, as though trying to remember. 'Peter Galliano.'

Hearing his partner's name aloud was like a small blow to the chest. 'Peter is . . .'. Spike pushed back his thick dark hair with a hand. 'He's unwell.'

The boy ran the toy along the wall again, then glanced slyly at his mother, mindful of her warning, testing her tolerance. Spike signalled to his office door, and she clasped her son's hand and led him inside, Spike following, nostrils protesting at the trail of cheap perfume. 'Please,' he said. 'Take a seat.'

The woman brushed a hand beneath her pencil skirt then lowered herself into the leather armchair. She was pale and petite and wore a dark fringe swept to one side. The gap between the sides of her thighs and the chair's arms seemed to scream Galliano's absence. As if sensing a lack, she scooped up her son and placed him on her lap, where he entertained himself by running the dinky car over his mother's knee. Spike shut his laptop so that he and the woman could make eye contact across the desk. 'It's about my husband,' she said.

The child made a soft revving sound at the back of his throat. Spike was about to reply that he was not that kind of lawyer when the woman broke in, 'You do know who he is?'

Spike smiled. 'I don't even know who you are, Mrs . . .'

'Grainger. My husband is . . . was . . . Simon Grainger.' She seemed to be expecting a reaction. Having failed to elicit one, she glanced down at her son, then looked at Spike guardedly with eyes as dark as her hair. 'His corpse was discovered on the Rock last month. By the Barbary macaques.'

Spike was touched by her ability to switch to a childproof register. He wondered if he'd made a hasty assumption based on the strength of her scent and the quality of her best skirt. He imagined his father, shaking his head, *We are all snobs to some degree, son* . . .

'I've been on sabbatical,' Spike replied, seeing the woman's cheeks bloom in embarrassment. 'I'm afraid I haven't kept up with the local news.'

The boy strained at his mother's grasp, then rolled off her lap and padded towards the French windows. They both watched in silence as he reached a fingertip to the glass, instinctively drawn to his own reflection. Spike cleared his throat, suddenly weary. 'What exactly did you want from Peter, Mrs Grainger?'

'Some help,' she said abruptly. 'The police claim my husband committed suicide. They've already closed the case.'

'And you feel . . .'

'Simon wouldn't . . .' Her voice came out in a whisper. 'He wouldn't have done that.'

'How can you be sure?'

Pink leaked like fuchsia ink into the skin of her neck. She pursed her lips, showing the first sign of a pucker, suggesting how she might look in ten years' time. Not too bad, Spike had to admit. 'Because of Charlie,' she said. 'Simon would never have abandoned his son.'

Spike noted that she didn't include herself in the reasons her husband might have had to stay alive. 'Did he leave a note?'

She threw him a scornful look. 'Of course not.' Then a pause: 'Listen, all I want is for someone to take a fresh look at what happened. I hoped your partner might find something that could make the police reopen the case.'

Just as Spike was about to reply, the boy turned away from the window. He had the same colouring and delicate features as his mother. His hands hung by his sides, toy car tightly grasped in one, chipped silver bonnet emerging.

The desk phone rang; Spike hit a button, but Galliano's mellifluous baritone was already rising from the machine, 'Congratulations on reaching the law office of Galliano & Sanguinetti . . .' An American voice followed: 'You'd better change up that message, sir . . .' Spike grabbed the receiver and gestured to Mrs Grainger, who beckoned to her son, then bent down to reaffix the velcro on one shoe.

'Thanks for coming back to me, Mr Clohessy,' Spike said, before switching the conversation to availability. In under a minute he'd secured an arrangement for them to meet the following day at Ocean Village Marina. As he hung up, Spike watched Mrs Grainger moisten a tissue on the tip of her tongue and dab it on her son's forehead. The boy had been leaning against the French windows. The panes were coated in dust.

'Look, I'll see what I can do, Mrs Grainger,' Spike said, conscious that a moment earlier he'd been about to give a different answer. 'I've got some contacts in the police. Let me ask around.'

The woman gave a shy smile. Her son looked up at her and then smiled too. She reached for her handbag.

'There'll be no charge for the preliminary enquiries,' Spike said. 'One thing, though,' he added as he held open the door. 'Why did you want to instruct Peter?'

Mrs Grainger turned. Her teeth were like porcelain, almost good enough to pass muster in Hollywood. 'I found his business card among my husband's papers.'

'I hadn't realised they'd met.'

'Nor had I. Goodbye, Mr Sanguinetti.'

The door closed. At Spike's ankles lay the rubbish bag from Peter Galliano's office, the bottle of rum bulging like prey in a snake's belly. When he opened the door to sling the bag outside, the Graingers were already gone.

Chapter Ten

The sun sank behind the Rock, the shopkeepers on Main Street finishing up for the day, crates of duty-free booze and fags sold, full-booted cars rejoining the long, hot frontier queues to Spain. In the Old Town behind, barbers and beauticians were opening for business, the locals celebrating the slight cooling of the August air with a swift French manicure or short back and sides.

Spike turned onto Irish Town, a street that took its name from the prostitutes who'd once used it as a shopfloor. 'I've never told my parents I'm a lawyer,' Galliano used to quip to clients. 'They still think I play piano in a brothel'. These days the street was full of shipping firms and accountants. Two long-established pubs gave it some life; as Spike passed the first – The Three Owls – he glanced in and saw a heavy-set man in a leather jacket staring back at him from the bar. The man was dark, Romani almost, with a prominent brow and thick stubble. He held Spike's eye unflinchingly, causing his breath to quicken and an unfamiliar panic to flutter in his chest.

'*Harampai*,' an old woman called out, 'you watch where you're going.' Spike started in shock, then put a hand to the woman's frail shoulder, steering her in the right direction. As she clattered away her shopping cart, he heard her mutter, 'Sanguinetti,' a threat perhaps that she might see fit to inform his father that he'd just been seen stumbling outside a pub. Inside the bar, the Romani was ordering a pint and flirting with the waitress. Spike shook his head, then turned up a set of stone steps leading to Line Wall Road.

A bus was waiting at the stop above, filling with passengers, most of whom shook the driver's hand as they got on, no money exchanged. One perk of life in Gibraltar: residents rode for free. A distant cousin waved at Spike as the bus rumbled off, heading for Both Worlds, the retirement village on the eastern side of the Rock.

Crossing Line Wall Road, Spike breathed in the warm sea air, trying to ease the paranoia that had dogged him since his return from Genoa. First Peter. Who would be next? And what would happen to Zahra, abandoned somewhere on the Gulf of Paradise?

To his left, a pair of enormous black cannons were ranged on the pavement, captured from the Russians during the Crimean War and awarded by the British to Gibraltar in recognition of her loyal service. Line Wall Road had once marked the end of the Rock, a two-mile stretch of protruding bastions, the Straits sloshing at their base. Since then, so much land had been reclaimed from the sea that the cannons were now aiming at the Morrisons mega-mart. Not a bad target, Spike thought, remembering the local shops that they'd put out of business.

No more military distractions: the glass and steel facade of St Bernard's Hospital loomed ahead. Spike took a final gulp of sea air, then stepped inside.

Chapter Eleven

The original hospital had been housed in a damp ex-military facility midway up the Rock. When the opportunity had come to relocate it, the planners must have been carried away by the possibilities of cheap reclaimed land, as the current site was vast, all glass-roofed corridors and empty, echoey wards. The only time capacity was likely to be reached, Spike thought as he passed a cobwebbed bust of Queen Elizabeth, was if there were a terrorist attack on the Rock. Perhaps that was what the authorities had had in mind.

The lifts were out of order, so Spike continued down a corridor of floor-to-ceiling windows giving onto a rear courtyard, where a wooden bench stood beside an oil drum teeming with fag butts. 'No Loitering', read a sign on the wall. Next came the Rehabilitation Unit, sponsored by Lionel Sacramento, owner of a chain of cigarette shops on the Rock, a man so wealthy he was rumoured to manage his money through his own hedge fund in London. Once past the mortuary – and its bank of drinks machines for the living – Spike had reached his destination, the ICU.

A nurse with standard-issue cheerful smile and dark ponytail glanced up from the desk. Spike caught a glimpse of the 'Facebook' logo before she minimised the screen. '*Indamai!*' she exclaimed in *yanito*. 'Your friend's a popular man today.'

'Not too late, am I?'

The nurse consulted her watch. 'Last visit is at 7.45 p.m. You're OK.'

She stood up and led Spike past the desk, smoothing her blue uniform over well-covered haunches. Clumsy acrylics of ships decorated the walls, each sponsored by a local company. An over-pressed air-conditioning unit hummed hoarsely.

The ward had eight beds, seven of them empty. In one corner, beside a window overlooking the smokers' courtyard, lay Peter Galliano. At least he would appreciate the view, reasoned Spike – Peter was a sixty-a-day man, after all.

'Well, come on,' the nurse cajoled.

Spike picked up a plastic chair from an empty bay. 'How is he today?' he asked, putting off the moment when he would have to look at Galliano's face.

'There's been no deterioration.'

'What do the doctors say?'

'He's been under for ten days. With a head trauma of this severity, I think we'd like to see him wake up quite soon.'

The whirr of Galliano's iron lung seemed to confirm this discouraging prognosis. The nurse tucked the sheets beneath his gowned body, running her hands down the heavy backs of his thighs. 'I was watching you the other day,' she said, bending in a way that Spike might have found provocative, had he been interested in picking up any signs. 'You should talk to him, you know. Not just sit there in silence. No one's sure yet how much they can understand.'

She drew out one of Peter's strong arms and checked the cannula affixed to the back of his hand. Written on the band was 'GALLIANO, PETER HORATIO; GHA 97739; 23-MAY-1959'. Spike smiled. He'd forgotten about Peter's middle name: Somerset and Horatio, they were quite the pair.

'Handover's at 8 p.m.,' the nurse said. 'You can stay till then.'

He nodded as she left, then scanned the empty bays, wondering who'd lain there recently, if anyone mourned them now. Finally he forced himself to look round. Beneath a heavily bandaged brow, Galliano's left eye was still grotesquely swollen, the bruise around it a yellowy-brown. The stubble merging into his goatee suggested the nursing staff had decided that a full beard would require less work. Spike noted with a little pleasure that the double chin had reduced. It's an ill wind, as Galliano might have joked.

'Hello, Peter.' Spike's voice sounded foolish. He glanced round, seeing the lights flicker then go out in the corridor behind. When he turned back, he focused on Galliano's good eye, its dark and rather beautiful lashes splayed below a trembling lid. 'I've been working on your cases, Peter . . .' He pressed on, telling him about the meeting he'd lined up with the CEO of Neptune Marine. He was about to mention the visit from the Grainger widow when he stopped. 'Listen, Peter,' he said, leaning in. 'I think it may be my fault you're in here.' He turned again, hearing a rapid squeak of rubber on linoleum. A long shadow spread across the doorway; he waited for the nurse to appear, but the shadow withdrew. Galliano's chest rose and fell in a slow mechanical rhythm. In the twilight, the rows of empty white beds took on an eerie hue.

Suddenly the footsteps returned, hurried and loud, as though someone were sprinting past the door, trying not to be seen. '*Hola?*' Spike called out, but no one replied. 'Hang on a sec, Pete,' he said, realising this was the first time he'd spoken naturally.

The nurses' station was empty. Handover already? What was it she'd said earlier? 'He's a popular man today.' Who else could have been visiting? Peter's sister had three young children, so she tended to come in the mornings while they were at school. The nurse wouldn't have been on shift then anyway. A clatter came from ahead as Spike moved down the corridor. Just around the corner was an amenity room – locked – and a patients' bath-room. He eased down the handle of the Gents and went inside.

The dying halogen bulb created an uncomfortable strobe on the ceiling. The door to the shower room hung open, cloudy water pooling on the coarse green plastic, smooth bars and handles fitted to assist the infirm. Alongside stood a toilet cubicle. The red-crescent dial read 'OCCUPIED'.

Spike crouched down, but found no feet beneath the frame. Feeling his pulse quicken, he straightened up and put a hand to the door. The clasp was engaged: pressing an ear to the plywood, he made out the tremor of controlled breathing and the slow, careful creak of a window being pulled open.

He slammed his shoulder against the door – 'Who's there?' – before a response came, '*Lo siento, lo siento* . . .' The dial rolled to 'Vacant', and Spike stepped back as a timid head peered round. A yellow-skinned youth in a hospital gown, standing on the lavatory seat, drip stand in one fist, fag-end quaking in the other.

Spike offered the boy a hand to help him down. 'Those things will kill you,' he said as the boy hurried away, drip stand rattling on the floor. I must be going mad, Spike thought to himself as he walked back to the ward, finding the nurse sitting at Galliano's bedside, scribbling onto his chart. 'Thought you'd gone home,' she said, lowering her biro. 'Listen, a few of us are going for a drink later in Casemates. If you're at a loose end . . .'

The idea of getting blitzed gave Spike's heart a momentary lift, until he imagined what it would be like to spend an evening surrounded by medics. 'Sorry. Got some work to do.'

The nurse gave a teasing frown. 'All work and no play . . .' she chided as she plumped the pillows. Spike looked again at Galliano's inert face. 'Thanks all the same,' he said as he walked away.

Chapter Twelve

The broad, new-build avenues of the Europort ceded again to the dark labyrinth of the Old Town. Spike thought back to Genoa, to the *caruggi* of the Porto Antico: at least it had been light in there. As he entered Bombhouse Lane, he felt the moist levanter breeze blow on the nape of his neck, ruffling his hair like a clammy hand. Ahead rose the facade of the Cathedral of St Mary the Crowned, the pavement outside it wide and uneven. Beneath the ground lay hundreds of corpses, mostly Genoese émigrés who'd paid to be buried close to the Cathedral at a time when the grave-yards were full and the Rock under siege. Spike had always dismissed them as superstitious fools, but now as he remembered a favoured line of his father's – *By night an atheist half believes in God* – he didn't feel quite so sure.

He glanced back down Main Street: in the half-light, the wrought-iron balconies and blue wooden shutters took on the air of a Riviera fishing village. The Genoese again – always the largest immigrant population in Gib – making their mark. Spike found his mind turning once more to Zahra. Would it have made a difference if he'd stayed in Italy a few days longer? He might have been just yards away from her, yet he'd jumped at the first chance to abandon his search and slunk back home.

Wiping the perspiration from his brow, he walked through the open doors of the Royal Calpe pub. Casey, the barmaid – crop-haired, peroxide blonde – glanced round from the muted TV. If Spike had hoped for a smile to lift his spirits he was to be disappointed.

'What'll it be?' Casey snapped.

'Pint of London Pride, please. And a vodka and tonic.'

She fixed the drinks, then snatched Spike's ten-pound note and turned back to a subtitled omnibus of *Coronation Street*.

Shaking his head, Spike moved deeper inside the pub. Though the decor remained resolutely 1970s British – fruit machines, cask ales, Sunday carvery, diamond-patterned glass above the bar – the real change had come in the clientele. Where once had sat tables of brawling squaddies, now just the occasional soldier or sailor perched alone, texting on a break from a training exercise. The former hordes of British expats – Tesco bags of Marmite and Heinz Baked Beans at their feet – had diminished to the odd leather-faced couple waiting for the frontier queues to ease before driving home to Marbs. Defence cuts, property crises . . . The one group still out in force were the locals. No longer mere tourist-industry workers, they now wore a uniform of power suits and silk blouses, rictus grins affixed as they explained to moon-faced Russians or anxious Italians exactly why their money would be safe on the Rock. Financial services had come to Gibraltar, and the natives – once in the employ of the British garrison – had adapted.

Spike's eye was caught by a lawyer from a rival firm, something of a high-flyer, people said. She was sitting with her back to a wall adorned by a series of hunting prints, a nod to the pub's name, The Royal Calpe, a Victorian foxhunt which had exploited a brief good period of Anglo-Spanish relations to secure permission to ride with hounds over the border. The lawyer was using the hunt to open a discussion on the political idiosyncrasies of Gibraltar, but seemed to be struggling with the etymology of 'Calpe'. 'It's a reference to the fact that the Rock has a hollow centre,' she said in her lilting Gibraltarian English. '"Mons Calpe" – "Hollow Mountain". It's Greek, I think. Or Latin . . .'

A few years ago, Spike might have taken the opportunity to join her and reveal that the word was actually Phoenician. Now he just sat back in his chair and drank his beer.

'Sorry I'm late.'

Spike looked up to find Jessica Navarro standing by his table. As usual, he'd forgotten how pretty she was: even in her white jeans and man's grey V-neck, the eyes of other drinkers were pulled towards her. Slung over her slim shoulder was a gym bag that he knew would contain her police uniform. She glanced down at his empty pint glass, then over at the vodka and tonic. 'Onto the chasers now?'

'It's for you.'

'Sorry. Let me get you another.'

'I'll do it . . .' He half-stood, but she was in no mood for indulging his old-fashioned chivalry and was already at the bar, where she drew a warmer greeting from Casey. By the time she returned, dropping her change into the British Red Cross collection box, Spike had stashed his empty glass on the shelf behind the table where the day's English papers lay half-read and abandoned.

'Out of sight, out of mind,' Jessica said.

Spike ignored her and took a gulp of his beer.

'So what's up?' she asked.

'How do you mean?'

'Summoned by Spike Sanguinetti for an evening drink?' She raised her dark, neatly curved eyebrows. 'To what do I owe the honour?'

Spike did his best at a smile, and she softened her tone: 'I'm worried about you, Spike. I haven't seen you like this in years.'

The oblique reference to the death of his mother provoked the usual feelings of exasperation. Then he recognised the real concern on Jessica's face, and checked himself. 'It's Peter, right?' she said, her tanned, heart-shaped face tilted to one side. A kink ran through her chestnut hair where it had been folded beneath her police hat. 'He could still wake up,' she added, and Spike gave a nod, aware that he could leave it at that. But he didn't. 'I don't think it was an accident, Jess.'

She sat back. 'Go on.'

'When I was in Genoa . . .' He watched Jessica's eyelashes flutter skywards in irritation. 'I told you I spoke to Zahra?'

'How could I forget.'

'Well, the man who took her. Žigon. He's not some small-time pimp. He's a serious player, the head of an organised crime syndicate. According to Interpol, he took out most of his rivals in the Balkans in a single night. Threw grenades through their windows. Six men – and their families – dead.'

Jessica nodded. 'I know all this. Drugs, people trafficking, prostitution. Said to run his operation out of the Italian Riviera.'

'Zahra warned me, Jess. Told me if I didn't back off, Žigon would hurt someone close to me.'

'Like your Dad?'

'Exactly.'

'Who's fine.'

'Or Peter. Who's not.'

Jessica took a sip of her drink, wincing at the flat, litre-bottle tonic.

'I'm pretty sure what happened to Peter is my fault,' Spike went on. 'Žigon sending me a message. A warning.'

'Why on *earth* would he do that?'

'As a punishment for getting too close to him. For trying to track down Zahra.'

Jessica carefully set down her glass. 'Let me get this straight, Spike. This Žigon, or whatever his name is, thinks you're on the verge of uncovering his real identity. So he sends someone to Gibraltar to run down your business partner.'

Spike nodded.

'While you're still in Italy.'

'Yes.'

'Presumably just a few miles away from where he lives.'

'Zahra says that's how he works.'

'Zahra says . . .' she mimicked, then downed her drink and forgot her scruples. 'Let's go through this step by step. Firstly, Peter

47

Galliano's accident was just that – an accident. We've had the lab results back from his blood sample. He was drunk, Spike. *Cagana*. Blotto.'

Spike thought of the empty bottle of rum in Galliano's bin.

'There was low cloud on the Rock that day. The driver might not have even known what he'd done. Might have thought he hit the kerb, or an ape. We don't know.'

'But you haven't found the driver.'

'Without CCTV, hit-and-runs take time to solve. The point is, Spike . . . this was not the work of a professional hit man. It was random and it was messy.'

He waited for her to continue.

'Secondly, this is Zahra we're talking about. I only met her a few times, but I can tell you this – she's the kind of woman who always lands on her feet. It doesn't surprise me in the least that she doesn't want you to look for her. When she first met you, she was a Bedouin refugee. No money, no papers. She would have done anything for an EU passport. You got her into Gib, then Malta. Now she's made it to Italy, to mainland Europe, the promised land. She's probably been given a new identity and doesn't want to be reminded of the old one. She's a born survivor, Spike. And she doesn't need you any more.'

'She was abducted, Jess.'

Jessica sighed. 'You don't know that.'

'I was there. In Malta. I know what happened.'

'Do you?' Her hand moved to his wrist, but he twisted it off. 'No one knows for certain that she was kidnapped. Did she say his name when you spoke to her? Did she ever use the word "Žigon"?'

Spike tried to remember.

'Listen, Spike. I've known you all my life. And ever since you met this girl things keep going wrong for you. Look at what you're doing. Listen to what you're saying. You're a commercial lawyer, not some vigilante trying to track down a homicidal crime lord.' Jessica paused, then spoke more gently. 'Your annoyingly beautiful ex-girlfriend has cut you off, and your business partner has had a terrible accident, but that's all there is to it. You've got to pull yourself together. Forget about Zahra and think of the future.' Her eyes were gleaming now. 'Don't you think I'm shaken up about Peter too? I'm doing everything I can to find out who was driving that car. There's a paint sample with forensics in London. We're getting the story out to Spain, OK?'

The pub door burst open, admitting the stubbled Romani Spike had seen in Irish Town. He carried a laundry bag, which he swung onto the bar, revealing a selection of handmade bangles. Casey picked one up admiringly, batting her false eyelashes.

'Spike?'

He looked back. 'A woman came to see me this morning. With a little boy. Her name was Grainger.'

'As in Simon Grainger?'

'You know her?'

'Hard not to. She was on the front page of the *Chronicle* for three days. Her husband killed himself, right?'

'Not according to her. And she's not too happy with the outcome of your investigation.'

'How do you mean?'

'She says the police closed the case with indecent haste.'

'Not our problem.'

'Why?'

'Redcaps.'

'What do they have to do with it?'

'The body landed just inside the base on the Rock. That makes it a military matter.'

'Even though Simon Grainger was a civilian?'

'Them's the rules, Spike. Thought you'd know that, Scholarship Boy.'

Spike half-smiled. 'Odd place to kill yourself, though, isn't it?'

'There's a flat bit of land above. Handy spot if you fancy ending it all. As long as you don't mind the gulls pecking out your eyes and the apes playing with your shattered limbs.'

Spike watched Jessica's cheeks colour as she remembered that the topic of suicide was not one Spike cared for. Then she shrugged and gave a conciliatory smile. 'Tell you what. I'll talk to the Chief Constable. They're lazy sods, the Redcaps. I'll see if they've cut any corners.' She reached behind for a menu. 'Now I need to eat something; it's been a long day.' Her lips pouted as she scanned the options – Calpe burger, egg and chips . . . 'It's good to see you watching out for the little people, though. That was why you went into law in the first place, wasn't it? To help out the underdog?'

Spike nodded, but as he walked back to the bar, he realised that he couldn't actually remember.

Chapter Thirteen

Spike turned into Chicardo's Passage, feeling the sweat from the climb sting the skin of his brow, suddenly aware that if Galliano ever did regain consciousness, Gibraltar had to be one of the worst places on Earth to find yourself confined to a wheelchair. The rows of dilapidated terraced houses stood just a few feet apart, the washing lines strung between them so short that only single items could be hung. Ahead, dangling against the night sky, Spike recognised a pair of his father's fraying brown cords.

He passed the house of his neighbours, Keith and Maeve Montegriffo, glancing as usual at the budgerigar in a metal cage wired to their first-floor balcony. The lights in his own kitchen were still on, he saw with a sigh, as he took out a gleaming Chubb key and pushed it into the newly fitted lock.

Any hopes that Rufus had left the lights on accidentally were dashed as Spike entered the hallway. 'An intruder perchance?' boomed his sardonic voice from the kitchen. 'Are we to be murdered in our beds?'

Spike placed his briefcase on the bottom stair. It was tempting to continue up, but instead he pushed heroically through the bead curtain.

Rufus Sanguinetti was sprawled in a wooden chair at the head of the table, a cafetière beside him, the plunger hopelessly skewed. He still insisted on brewing Nescafé inside Spike's Christmas present. A mug lay at his elbow, a copy of the *Gibraltar Chronicle* open in front of him. '"Asterisk betrayal",' Rufus called out. 'Six – comma – five.'

'You're up late, Dad.'

Without bothering to look up from his crossword, Rufus extended a long arm towards a tea crate beneath the dresser. It hadn't been there this morning. 'Found it by the immersion heater. Wants sorting.'

'You shouldn't be up in the attic by yourself.'

'Murderers up there, are there? Should we put a stronger chain on the door? Drill a spy hole?'

Rufus lifted his large, leonine head and appraised Spike, caressing the side of his Roman nose with a tapering finger. 'You haven't been in the pub, have you?'

'Working late.'

Spike gave his father's shoulder an awkward squeeze, then filled a glass from the tap. Cringing at the tepid minerality of Gibraltar's new desalination plant, he found his eyes ranging over the contents of the crate. Photographs, diaries, letters – Rufus's compulsion to indulge in nostalgia was becoming a concern. Spike reached inside for a pack of blue airmail letters, recognising with a jolt of sadness his mother's handwriting, with its earnest mix of capitals and underlinings.

'Now come along,' Rufus said, returning to the newspaper. 'Final clue, fourteen down . . .'

Spike stared across at him, taking in the white hair flowing over his shoulders like an ageing prophet's. Ever since the death of his wife, Rufus had insisted on being his own barber. His strong forehead was furrowed with concentration above his spectacles, fitted with a hearing aid now, kept at an incredibly high sensitivity. Thin, pale forearms protruded from his short-sleeved shirt, draped over the table like vegetable stalks forced in the dark. In one corner lay a dog basket full of newspapers, the crossword of each indented with hard-pressed biro answers.

'Double-cross,' Spike said.

Rufus narrowed his eyes behind his half-moons as Spike held out a hand: 'Sorry?'

Reluctantly the chewed biro was released. In the blank space to the side of the page, Spike marked out a cross, then scored another over the top at an angle. An asterisk was formed. 'Double-cross,' Spike repeated, failing to keep the amazement from his voice. Normally he was more of a quick crossword man.

'No need to shout,' Rufus said, adjusting his hearing aid as he filled in the answer. 'There. Boy's a genius. Always said so.' He shunted his chair back, then tossed the newspaper into the dog basket. Both father and son stared down for a moment. It had been empty of its occupant for four months now. 'Come on, Dad. Let's get you upstairs.'

With painful slowness, Rufus clambered to his feet. His condition was worsening, but as long as he could still make the climb to bed on his own, Spike felt there was hope. As he followed his father out of the kitchen, he scooped up the slim pack of age-softened letters from the top of the crate and slipped them into his inside pocket. With Jessica's assurances fresh in his mind, he left the door on the latch for the first time in weeks, then fell in behind Rufus on the stairs.

Chapter Fourteen

A patch of damp rot decorated the wall above Spike's bed, a brown and taupe mosaic he'd loved to stare at as a boy, searching it for exotic shapes like a cloud-spotter. Pulling off his suit jacket, he sat down at his childhood desk, still defaced by the compass scratches and pen marks of his schooldays. *A girl who always lands on her feet* . . . Was that really the Zahra he knew? Could she simply have left Malta for her own reasons? Met someone else? Someone who had helped her get into Italy?

Disgusted at how easy it was to find the worst in people, particularly if it suited you, Spike opened his briefcase and took out his papers. Top of the pile was the list of questions he'd compiled for Morton Clohessy, CEO of Neptune Marine. Spike made a few notes, then reached across for the window, creaking up the rotten sash and seeing the terracotta rooftops of the Old Town undulating below, the Straits beyond, ships' lights flashing along the lanes of traffic as they ferried their cargoes from Atlantic to Mediterranean, Mediterranean to Atlantic.

He put down his pen and picked up the sheaf of letters from the bed. Something had been niggling at him, he realised as he leafed through the bundle: the top envelope was addressed in his mother's hand, yet she was also the recipient – Mrs Rufus Sanguinetti, 12 Chicardo's Passage, Gibraltar. Too long ago for postcodes. The stamp looked French; he worked the envelope from its cotton binding, finding it carefully opened with a knife, then checked the date: May 23rd 1977. Spike had been three.

'*Dear J,*' the letter began. Could you invade a dead person's privacy? Probably, Spike thought, but read on anyway.

'*Last week we arrived in La Rochelle. The Bay of Biscay is as clean and beautiful as I remember, but the town is clogged with tourist cafés and discotheques . . .*' Spike had no memory of La Rochelle; the family holidays he recalled had always been in Portugal, on the beaches of the central Algarve. '*I suppose that I have changed as well. Whereas before I would have wanted to explore, to ask questions, now I find it hard to make myself leave the hotel terrace, sitting here smoking these horrible French cigarettes while R and S busy themselves around me. S in particular brings such joy. He's such a carefree, open little boy, gazing up at me with his bright blue eyes. Burnt brown already by the sun, just like I used to be. Whenever I watch him, I can't help but smile. Yet my heart is full of you, my J, my love . . .*'

Who the hell was 'J'? Suddenly ashamed, Spike stopped reading and pushed the delicate blue parchment back into its envelope. Look to the future, Jessica had said. He shut the package into his desk drawer and walked next door to the bathroom.

Staring back from the mirror was the image of a competent professional, restored on his return from Genoa by the attentions of the most expensive barber on Victualling Office Lane. The whites of his eyes were clear; even his crooked nose now seemed to suit the planes of his dark, angular face. He stepped into the shower, drenching the tense muscles of his neck and shoulders in the steamy heat. Cooled by a fresh white T-shirt, he stretched out on his bed and stared up at the wall, trying not to run through the possibilities of who 'J' might be.

Ten minutes later, he flicked on his phone. A text had just come in with an Italian prefix. The words were in English: '*Sr and Sra Radovic have reservation for Presidential Suite next week. For small fee, I take photo on my camera phone? Your family friend, Enrico (of Hotel Splendido)*'.

Spike sat up. He'd forgotten about Enrico Sanguinetti. If Jessica's reading of Galliano's accident was right, and Žigon really posed no threat, then what was the harm in Enrico sending a picture of him and Zahra together?

'If the photo is clear, that's 100 euros for your daughter's fund', Spike texted back. He hit send, then lay back and closed his eyes, finding sleep closer than at any point in the last six months.

*

My father always distrusted the English. Self-serving cabrones, he would say dismissively while I was studying the language at school. A mask of courtesy constructed to hide their duplicity and greed. The Spanish had religious zeal to justify their hunger for Empire. But the English?

I cross the sitting room and examine the bookshelves, running a fingertip along the spines of the Golden Age literature so lovingly collected by my parents – Cervantes, de Vega, Calderón de la Barca. Surveying the furniture of the apartment, I admire the cherrywood console, the silver carriage clock, the exquisite tea caddies which were a particular favourite of my mother's. The last item I had to sell was an exceptional eighteenth-century walnut dresser, the empty space still prominent beneath the portrait of my ancestor, the great de Guzmán, Terror of Peru. I feel duty to family tug once more. Deber: something owed. If I take this Gibraltar job, I may never need to sell again.

I turn to assess myself in the colonial sunburst mirror. The carefully manicured stubble will have to go. As will the bull's-blood leather brogues and soft, lemon-yellow cashmere jumper knotted around my shoulders. Hernán once told me: Go to a café. Look around. Describe each person in a single phrase. 'The woman with the bare midriff'; 'The man in the string vest'. You need to be the person who defies description. The man with . . . ?

From the next door room I hear the chink of bottles. I smile to myself and move to the kitchen.

The waiter turns as I walk in. Three hours I waited for him in the Plaza Mayor. Now I can't remember his name. He stares back at me, and I read the lust in his eyes.

'Some of your mixers were out of date, like, last decade,' *he says, raising his metal eyebrow bolt in mock disapproval.*

I shrug apologetically as he pulls off his gilet, revealing a scooped white T-shirt beneath, his biceps defiled with cheap black ink, crowns of thorns around the muscles. Appropriate, I think, taking a step closer.

'I was going to make us cocktails,' the waiter murmurs, turning back to the drinks tray, trainers crinkling the newspaper I have laid beneath, 'but as you only have local spirits, I'm going to fix you, my rudest customer of the year . . .'

Slowly I draw the retractable truncheon from my pocket, glancing back at the kitchen table to see if the queer has been drinking. Good, a glass or two of brandy already. With a swift flick of the wrist I extend the truncheon to its full length. The waiter turns again, and I watch confusion, then fear, flood into his eyes before I bring the heavy steel shaft down on the crown of his head.

The glass slips from the waiter's grasp as he falls sideways to the floor. I step towards him, flipping him onto his back so that his head rests on a copy of El País. *The sports section, I note with irritation. As I kneel down, I hear rasping breaths, faster and faster. 'What . . .' he is trying to say '. . . why?'*

I peer downwards. The blow has cracked the top of his skull perfectly. I know that beneath the teased strands of bleached hair will lie a web of hairline fractures, like a frozen pond struck with a hammer. I grip the truncheon in both hands. He is whimpering now, like a kitten in a sack. As soon as the truncheon is correctly positioned, I jab downwards at his fontanelle and feel the tip plunge deep into the centre of his brain.

All four of his limbs start twitching. I am reminded of a rare time it snowed in Madrid, making snow angels as a boy. Was that me or a character from a childhood book? I withdraw the truncheon, spilling not a drop of blood, and walk over to the sink, where I rinse a series of soft pearly flecks from the shaft.

The little insect is still quivering on the floor. Suddenly I feel rejuvenated, twenty years younger. The old city haunts come flashing back to my mind – the beauty spots, the hills outside the suburbs, all the places a drunk fag looking for company might slip and find himself in trouble. I remember Hernán's face as he analysed me in the restaurant – 'Are you sure you're still up to it?' *– and smile.*

Lifting an old roll of carpet out of the utility room, I wrap the still shivering body inside and begin my clean-up. Then I take out my phone and text Hernán – 'Standing by.'

Chapter Fifteen

The RIB eased its way out of Ocean Village. Once past the Detached Mole, the driver gunned the engine, glancing back as the waves started to smash against the inflatable stern, spattering the only passenger's sky-blue shirt with navy. Spike smiled, heeling his briefcase beneath his seat and raising his head, enjoying the cool salty spray on the underside of his neck. The driver turned back to sea with a hint of disappointment.

As the boat powered along the western side of Gibraltar, Spike took in the familiar landmarks – the flat, reclaimed land where Peter Galliano lay in his hospital bed; the houses of the Old Town, huddled on the limestone like survivors of a shipwreck; then the Rock, rising out of the water, resplendent against the horizon like an ancient lion, the dark mouths of tunnels pockmarking its flanks, some dating from the eighteenth century, providing flanking fire against Spanish besiegers, others from the Second World War, when the rubble extracted had been hastily used to build Gibraltar's tiny airport runway. A flag flew at the peak – a red castle, a golden key and the motto 'Montis Insignia Calpe', *Sign of the Hollow Mountain.*

Spike thought back to his drink with Jessica at the Royal Calpe. That was what friends did, told you what you didn't want to hear, stuck by you even when you were terrible company. It wasn't as if Jessica had had an easy time of it herself lately. But they never seemed to talk about that.

Feeling a sudden surge of affection for Jessica, Spike turned to the view in front. Europa Point marked the southernmost tip of the Rock, a red-and-white lighthouse projecting at its edge, warning the shipping traffic of the hidden dangers of the Straits – 'that awful deepdown torrent', as Molly Bloom had summed it up in *Ulysses*. Opposite, Spike could make out Jebel Musa, one of the twin guardians of the mouth of the Mediterranean. To the Romans, these mountains – one in Europe, one in Africa – had represented the Pillars of Hercules, the *non plus ultra* beyond which sailors would drop off the end of the earth into a void of eternal damnation. As their floating destination came into view, Spike found himself wondering if the Romans hadn't had a point.

The ship was over a hundred feet long, her broad industrial hull covered in a newish coat of dark green paint. A converted cargo vessel, Spike guessed, the unassuming appearance perhaps intended to draw attention away from the hi-tech satellite system built into her mast. Stencilled in large black letters on one side was her name, *Trident*.

The driver accelerated into one last wave, then steered the RIB around the *Trident*. The ensign was one Spike was seeing more and more of in Gib, usually on a gin palace or superyacht. A red background with a green turtle on one side and a Union Jack on the other – the flag of the Cayman Islands.

A set of metal-mesh steps was flipped down by two thickset men, both wearing the same navy polo shirts as the driver, a three-pronged fork monogrammed in yellow silk on the breast pocket. As Spike made his way down the RIB, he stumbled in the swell and felt a gnarled hand catch his wrist. The driver stared into his eyes, a Scot, judging by the few words he'd said when he'd picked Spike up, though his olive skin suggested Italian heritage. Despite his sober demeanour – clean-shaven, short hair – his eyes had a bloodshot glaze Spike knew well. 'Watch yourself, eh?' he warned as Spike gripped his briefcase in one hand and the frame of the steps in the other. The amused look rankled.

Why was it that a person was assumed to have lost all physical competency as soon as they put on a suit?

Declining further help aboard, Spike pulled himself onto the deck of the *Trident*, seeing the RIB hurtle away behind him towards Gibraltar Harbour, the driver revealing how he preferred to travel when not inconvenienced by landlubbers. When Spike looked back, a man was walking towards him across the varnished deck. The easy stride and aura of authority suggested this must be Morton D. Clohessy.

No longer in a moving vessel, Spike suddenly felt the midday sun pounding on his head. 'Mr Sanguinetti,' Clohessy called out as his colleagues slipped like mice below deck. He was tall and lean, the tanned skin of his face stretching around a square jaw, tinted glasses resting on his pointed nose. A receding hairline had left a brown island of hair marooned on his brow. Everything about him seemed practical and expensive: the soft grey trainers, the wipe-clean Rohan jacket, the photochromic lenses, the mobile phone sheathed at his side like a knife. He looked about forty, but was probably ten years older. 'Mort Clohessy,' he said. 'Welcome aboard.' The handshake was the predictable bonecrusher, though the smooth palm belied his all-weather uniform. 'You're taller than I imagined,' he said. 'What are you, one ninety?'

'Sorry – I only operate in imperial units.'

'A true Brit, after all.' He smiled. 'Please, follow me.'

A gantry crane rose at the stern of the boat, with an alcove below, fitted with two padded white seats. Clohessy ushered Spike into one, then sat down beside him, the cushion responding with a gasp of stale air. 'I thought we might sit up here for a while, if you don't mind.'

Spike nodded affably as the boat pitched from side to side.

'I spend too much time below deck.'

A creaking came from above, and Spike glanced up at the crane, as black and forbidding as a gallows. A reel was attached to its upper beam, a rope arrowing downwards to the lower deck.

Spike followed it with his eyes and saw that it ran through another reel, then into the water, rigid yet moving, as though playing a shark. 'That's the cable for our ROV,' Clohessy said. 'Remotely Operated Vehicle. Robot on a string, basically. Originally built to lay deepwater fibre-optic cable on the seabed. We bought and modified her at a cost of some four million dollars.' He paused to allow the figure to sink in. 'Eight side-thrusters, six underwater cameras giving constant feeds of the seabed. Fifteen thousand dollars a day to run.' His low voice had a nasal American accent with a twang of something Spike couldn't place.

'Wouldn't divers be cheaper?' Spike asked.

One of Clohessy's sparse eyebrows shot into his wide expanse of brow. 'We've moved on a bit since Jules Verne, Mr Sanguinetti. Anyway, it's too deep to dive this side of the reef.' He placed a tanned, wiry hand on Spike's arm. 'How is your partner? Any sign of improvement?'

'I'm afraid Peter is still in a coma. The prognosis is not good.'

Clohessy made a clicking noise with his tongue. 'Pressing on like this – it seems wrong. But with the costs at stake . . .'

'You instructed Galliano & Sanguinetti, Mr Clohessy. I'll do everything I can to fulfil the brief.'

Clohessy's smile revealed two rows of small, tightly packed teeth. 'I appreciate your attitude. Now, let's get down to it.'

Chapter Sixteen

Any remnants of the *Trident*'s humble origins vanished as Spike descended the narrow staircase into the hold. The guts of the ship had been eviscerated, creating a central open-plan space flickering with high-definition monitors and wafer-thin computer screens. Spike was introduced to the key members of Neptune's team, all quietly working away, all sporting the same monogrammed polo shirts – Jamie, a marine archaeologist cultivating an unconvincing goatee; Stevo, a South African 'MacGyver' whose job was to engineer devices to raise awkward items of salvage; Anders, a Swede who did something with 'bathymetric sonar', and Mike, a bald American who was maintaining the position of the boat using only a computer keyboard.

In front of the largest screen sat a dark-haired youth, face pitted with unhealed acne scars. His hands were plunged into black, elbow-length rubber gloves, with which he appeared to be controlling the movements of a metal pincer moving through a murky green space. Spike assumed this was some kind of video-game simulation until a school of sea bream flashed past the screen. 'Watch your tail, Johnnie,' Clohessy snapped, pointing at the umbilical cord that connected the robot to the boat. Johnnie waved his arms to one side and the pincer pressed on into the algae-clouded gloom.

'Johnnie's flying our ROV for the morning,' Clohessy said to Spike. 'You met our senior pilot earlier.'

'Did I?'

'Johnnie's brother. He picked you up in the RIB.'

'He wasn't one for introductions.'

'That'd be Dougie,' Johnnie murmured in a Scottish accent as he steered the robot past a pile of silt-covered girders.

Clohessy sat down, inviting Spike to do the same. His photochromic glasses had grown clearer the further they'd descended into the ship, revealing a pair of shrewd shark's eyes set close together beside the sharp nose. 'You've done your fair share of treasure work, I imagine,' he said.

Just call the boat 'she' and you'll be fine, had been Galliano's advice on shipping cases. 'Not really,' Spike said, sensing a few heads turn.

'But you're familiar with the nature of modern salvage?'

'I have a working knowledge of admiralty law.'

Clohessy's irritation was clear, yet his voice remained controlled. 'Let's start with the basics, then,' he said. 'As I was telling you earlier, the era of scuba divers and oxygen tanks is over. Anders over there spends the winter months on our scout ship, the *Triton*, shooting sonar over potential wreck sites that Jamie' – the man with the weak goatee raised a hand – 'finds by checking the Hydrographic Database against old copies of *Lloyd's List*.'

'Amongst other sources,' Jamie called out in an English public-school voice.

Clohessy threw him an impatient look. 'If Anders picks up a man-made anomaly, we wait until summer, then call in the *Trident* and send down the ROV. If there are traces of a shipwreck, we'll check first for diagnostic artefacts – a cannon, say, or an anchor. Failing that, we can carbon-date timber or ballast to get a sense of when she sank. Once we've confirmed the identity of the ship, we try and find her cargo. Then and only then do we make our legal application to salvage.'

'Which you did last month to the Receiver of Wreck.'

'Correct.'

'Felix Canessa has been receiver in Gibraltar for over ten years. Captain of the Port for fifteen. I don't see why he needs a judge to decide the matter.'

'Johnnie?' Clohessy said, a first tremor of excitement entering his voice.

The pilot parted his gloved hands and the image on the screen broadened out.

'The older the wreck, the more scattered the cargo. For the *Gloucester* . . .'

'The *Gloucester*?'

Clohessy's tone took on a brittle edge. 'You didn't read the file?'

'It's referred to as "The Wreck" throughout the documentation,' Spike replied crisply.

Clohessy gave an ungracious nod as Jamie hit a button on his keyboard to reveal a close-up of a seaweed-encrusted ship's hull. Faintly visible on the metal were four letters, 'GLOU'.

'That's handy,' Spike said.

Smiling again, Clohessy reached for a plastic bag lying on the white work surface. He unsealed it and took out a rusty fork, its handle knobbled with tiny barnacles. 'Ivory,' he said proudly, holding up the implement by a string tag. 'Carbon-datable to within a single year of when the elephant was shot. Mid-nineteenth century, bang on the money for the *Gloucester*.' He dropped the fork back into its bag like a court exhibit.

'So what's the receiver worried about?'

Clohessy unzipped his mackintosh; no polo shirt for him, just a T-shirt marked *Whistler*, one half of a maple leaf etched above. Canada . . . of course, not American at all. 'The *Gloucester* was a British freighter,' he said, tugging out his T-shirt to cool his washboard chest. 'Her manifest records that she was transporting armaments to British troops during the Crimean War. On 24th August 1853 she set sail back to Southampton carrying a cargo of Ukrainian lead ingots. On her way into Gib for bunkering, she got snagged on the Europa Reef, which is starboard of where we are now – the size of another Rock of Gibraltar, Anders tells us, hidden just below the surface.' The Swede nodded his white-blond head like an obedient labrador. 'We've found over three tons of the lead already, which is pretty good going. Johnnie?' Clohessy called out, and Spike saw the Scotsman tense his scarred jaw, perhaps keen to make the most of his opportunity to shine while his elder brother was away. The screen switched to what Spike had assumed were girders. On closer inspection, he saw that the rods were made of smaller individual bars encrusted together.

Clohessy snapped his fingers. 'More to the left,' he said as a larger heap of barnacled metal appeared. An octopus retreated into a gap; Johnnie extended the ROV's pincer into its lair and it pulsed away, squirting a sac of ink. He glanced again at Clohessy, hoping in vain for a nod of approval.

'Four million pounds for some scrap metal?' Spike said.

'A conservative estimation.'

'Why so much?'

'The lead is low-alpha,' Clohessy replied matter-of-factly as he waved the ROV further to the left.

'That means nothing to me.'

Clohessy's sinewy neck whipped round. There was something raptorial in his face, Spike thought, as though at any moment he might lean forward and take your eyes. 'Did you hear that?' he called to the rest of the crew. 'Intellectual honesty. You can all learn from that.' He stared down at Spike, arms folded across his T-shirt. 'I run a no-bullshit operation here,' he said, and now Spike could see the ruthlessness that had helped him make his first fortune – something complicated in tech, according to Google. 'No booze and no bullshit. Those are my rules aboard this ship.' Clohessy turned back to the screen, brow unwrinkling like a sandbank smoothed by the tide. 'From the moment lead is mined, its molecular makeup alters. Lead that's over a hundred

and fifty years old will degrade to a point where its alpha parti-
cles diminish. That makes it ideal for use in the semiconductor
industry.' He reached into his holster and drew out his BlackBerry;
flipping off the rubber back, he pointed at a skinless electronic
carcass. 'The chip in this device runs on low-alpha lead. Regular
lead gives off low-level radiation that interferes with the electron-
ics. The low-alpha type is silent – which is why it retails at up to
a thousand dollars a pound. From shipwreck to Smartphone,' he
concluded with a grin that suggested a fondness for the phrase.
'So that's our salvage. A decent, medium-sized commodities hit
for Neptune.' He paused and gave a wink. 'But not enough to
drag *me* all the way from Vancouver.' All faces in the ship's office
were now fixed on Clohessy's. 'More to the right,' he said to
Johnnie. 'Stop there.'

What looked like a discarded steel washing machine lay at an
angle on the seabed. It was hard to get a sense of scale, until a
conger eel writhed obligingly past. A square of metal had been
sliced from the box; with admirable agility, the ROV pincer nosed
its way in through the gap. The screen switched to infrared as the
interior of the box became visible.

'More lead ingots?' Spike said.

Clohessy's eyes were bright. 'Not exactly,' he replied, sliding
open a drawer in the workstation. 'We brought this up last week.'
He handed Spike a glinting bar of metal, no bigger than a Mars
Bar. The shine and weight suggested solid silver.

'Ah,' Spike said.

'Ah indeed.'

It was tempting to put the bar to his mouth, test it with his
teeth as they did in the movies. Instead Spike laid it gently back
down on the desk and stared at it. 'This complicates matters.'

'Naturally.'

'Was the silver listed on the outward manifest?'

Clohessy shook his head. 'The safe was in the captain's cabin. Our
best guess is that he was moving it in secret to avoid excise duty.'

'Smuggled silver bullion ...' Spike said. 'The *Gloucester* was part of the British merchant navy, right?'

'Yes.'

'So if she sank during wartime, and was commandeered to supply troops, that makes her a sovereign vessel.'

Clohessy shrugged.

'In which case the MoD will own the cargo.'

'The *listed* cargo.'

Spike paused, thinking. 'Or customs might have a claim.'

'Might?'

'Or it could be a case of "finders keepers".'

'That's about where we'd got to with Paul.'

'Paul?'

'Your partner?'

'Peter,' Spike said sharply, and Clohessy made an attempt at a respectful nod.

'Have you told the MoD about this?' Spike asked.

As if on cue, voices murmured outside. The hatchway opened and Dougie, the RIB driver, reappeared, fists strung with plastic shopping bags. Stooped behind him was a tall, rigid figure Spike vaguely recognised. 'Thought this was meant to be state of the art,' the man said disparagingly, before taking in the flashing lights of the control room and adjusting his assessment. 'Hugh Jardine,' he declared as he walked towards Spike. 'MoD. Military Liaison Officer.' He stopped and gave a practised grin. 'Haven't we met before?'

Chapter Seventeen

A table appeared at the rear of the central cabin, swiftly and noiselessly assembled by Stevo, as Dougie laid out the unimaginative buffet he'd brought from Morrisons – pap white bread, a wheel of Dairylea, a few unappealing tubs of hummus and slabs of pâté. Spike thought ruefully of what was available on the Rock to those in the know – sweet pastrami from Idan's, crisp falafel from Samir's . . .

Mike, the American, remained faithfully at his station, battling the currents of the Straits to keep the *Trident* in place while everyone else sat down around the table, with Spike positioned – inevitably, he felt – between Clohessy and Jardine.

The Neptune workers ate efficiently and said little, preferring to listen to Jardine being brought up to speed on the latest developments of the salvage. 'Now that's what I call a silver lining,' Jardine said eventually. Spike gave a stiff smile at the weak joke, then began: 'The key matter to address is that of apportionment.'

'No legalese,' Jardine groaned, 'I beg of you.'

Spike shot the soldier a sideways glance. He'd seen him around the Rock over the years, but had assumed he must have retired by now. He wore blue chinos and a pink shirt redolent of old cologne and cigarette smoke. His lips were cracked and his cleft chin had run to fat, but it was the eyes Spike recognised, narrowed and knowing, as though enjoying some private longstanding joke.

Feeling the weight of Spike's stare, Jardine turned. A strand of his mousy hair had worked itself from its bed of pomade and hung dankly over his forehead. Too long for a military man, Spike decided, pegging him as a smooth talker with a Sandhurst education and flat feet. 'I understand Neptune has contracted with the Ministry of Defence to split the salved fund sixty-forty.'

'In Neptune's favour,' Clohessy retorted at once.

'Can you confirm that the MoD is happy to retain these terms given the additional potential value of the silver, Mr Jardine?'

'Captain Jardine' – the grey eyes twinkled in their narrow shells – 'will endeavour to find out.'

'In which case we can return to the main issue. I feel there's a good chance that the judge will rule that the silver was illegally imported. If that happens, he may confiscate it in favour of the Crown.'

'You *feel* there's a chance?' Jardine echoed, seeking Clohessy's eye. 'Doesn't sound too convincing, does it?'

Spike ignored him. 'What we have to do is persuade the judge to see the salvage as a case of "finders keepers". The danger then is of an heir to the original owner of the silver emerging, which, judging by that unmarked bar' – Clohessy had already shown Jardine his discovery – 'is unlikely.'

Clohessy nodded. 'Initial tests suggest the silver came from a mine in southern Ukraine. The captain probably acquired it on the sly, so we don't believe there will be any trace documents.'

'That remains to be seen. The point is that the more favourably the judge looks upon Neptune Marine and its operations, the more likely he will be to award you the silver. He needs to believe that you merit this windfall. Everything must be done by the book.' Spike turned again to Jardine. 'Hence why you need to talk to your superiors at the MoD as a matter of urgency.'

Jardine sank a corner of bread into a beige tub of hummus and pushed it between his purple lips. Clohessy watched him with barely concealed disgust, then shoved his own plate away untouched. Catching sight of the raised veins on his arms, Spike wondered if he was ill, or had a complicated relationship with food. 'Excuse me, gentlemen,' Clohessy said. 'I have to make a call.' As soon as he was gone, Jardine reached for the glass bottle on the table, but was disappointed to find it contained only water. A film of moisture covered his face, like cheddar left out of the fridge overnight. 'When do you need an answer?' he said.

'The hearing's on Monday.'

'Friday, then?'

'At the very latest.'

Jardine drained his cup then assessed Spike's face. 'You don't have a musician in the family, do you? A mother? An aunt?'

Spike felt his instinctive dislike of the man harden. 'The former.'

'That must be why you look so familiar. I'm sure your mother gave my eldest violin lessons. Must have been ... what, eighteen years ago? She used to come to our house after school. Name of ... Missoni?'

'Mifsud.'

'Mifsud ... Well, well, well.' He laughed, stroking what remained of his cleft chin. 'But you're a Sanguinetti, I thought?' He kept the 'g' hard in the local Gibraltarian way – San-*ghin*-etti. Really must have been on the Rock a while.

'My mother taught under her maiden name.'

'Never forget a face,' Jardine said, nodding contentedly as he chewed. 'It's a useful skill out here, of course, given how close the community ...' He let the sentence fall, with its innuendoes of interbreeding.

'You two rubbing along?' Clohessy murmured to Spike as he arrived back at the table.

'Finding common ground,' Jardine said.

'What was it you were saying the other day, Hugh? Thirty thousand locals? In an area of six square kilometres?'

'It is indeed a small world, Mort,' Jardine replied.

'How about Simon Grainger?' Spike said. 'Did you come across him?'

Something in Spike's tone caused a hush to fall around the table. Jardine smiled and continued eating. 'What about him?' he asked, spraying pink crumbs of pâté into the close air.

'His widow came to see me,' Spike said. 'She thinks the military police botched the investigation into his death.'

The silence that followed was oppressive. Clohessy shifted in his chair as a team member scrambled to revive an earlier conversation. A Gibraltarian had recently taken the crown in the Miss World contest; apparently the mix of émigré races on the Rock had worked to create an exceptionally beautiful local population.

'Your client is mistaken,' Jardine resumed.

'In what way?'

'I imagine she didn't mention the pathologist's report.'

'Was that a military pathologist?'

Jardine either missed or ignored the tone. 'There was a cocktail of antidepressants in the man's blood, Spike. Cipramil. Zoloft. Poor sap. We thought it best kept out of the press for the family's sake.' He shot Spike another glance. 'It's not easy for a child when a parent commits suicide.'

The tension was punctured by a shout from the other side of the cabin. 'Sir,' Mike the American called to Clohessy, 'our Spanish friends are back.' He tapped at his keyboard and the monitor switched to a view from the *Trident*'s topmast. Approaching from the south was a police speedboat, a grey machine gun mounted on its rear deck. Spike recognised the red and gold livery of the Guardia Civil.

''Kin 'ell,' Dougie muttered, getting to his feet. 'Third time this week.'

'What's the problem?' Jardine asked, looking from face to face.

'Spanish coastguards,' Clohessy replied. 'They say we're trespassing in their waters.'

Jardine gave a snort. 'Typical *Slopis*. Whole country's on its uppers so they have to pirate British waters.'

72

'This will be about the Estrecho Oriental,' Spike said.

'That's what they've been saying on the loudhailer. What does it mean?' asked Clohessy.

'It's a marine nature reserve. The Spanish refuse to recognise the existence of Gibraltarian waters. They claim they now have legal backing from the EU, as the European Court of Justice unwittingly passed a motion declaring that half our waters fall within a Spanish conservation area.'

Mike tapped at the microphone, preparing to make an announcement over the *Trident's* speaker system.

'It's specious,' Spike went on. 'Any state recognised by the UN has jurisdiction over at least three nautical miles off its own shore. That takes precedence over any so-called nature reserve.'

'Wait,' Clohessy called to Mike. 'We have a lawyer aboard. Let's see what he can do.'

Spike shrugged, then stepped forward to the microphone. He spoke in fluent Spanish, hearing his words reverberate tinnily above deck. On screen, the camera showed the patrol boat slow down, then circle the *Trident* aggressively before speeding away towards the Spanish mainland. A cry of triumph went up from the Neptune team.

'What did you say to them?' Clohessy asked, slapping Spike on the back.

'That we were filming them for a report commissioned by the European Court of Justice.'

'Was that all?'

'And that I knew where the driver lived in Algeciras.'

'Do you?'

'All the Guardia boys come from there. It's a racket.'

Clohessy laughed. 'You've earned your fee, son. Wouldn't get Paul pulling that stunt.'

'Peter,' Spike said icily. 'His name is Peter Galliano.'

Dougie picked up Spike's briefcase. 'Allow me to run you back to the Rock, sir.'

As Spike climbed back up to the upper deck, Jardine stopped him, laying a yellowed finger on his arm. 'Beautiful girl, your mother. Such a shame.'

*

Queues. Never-ending queues. I swelter in the uncomfortable seat of my cramped SEAT Ibiza, driver's window down. Everywhere I see these strange number plates, brief as swear-words – G6935, G4482. It's like stepping back in time. The booking line of my hotel had just five digits. Five!

The delivery van in front – Gibraltar plates – is being searched by Spanish customs, the belly of the official straining to escape the buttons of his nylon shirt. I want to pull out of the queue and gut him. Grizzled, wall-eyed – clearly the local junta *puts the real cretins on border duty. At last, after finding nothing more sinister than some trays of wilting lettuce, the official gives the van the nod to proceed.*

As the driver gets back into his cabin, he stares pointedly at my Madrid number plate. A moment later, a hand emerges from the window to dump the heaped contents of an ashtray onto Spanish soil. I see a beaming face in his rear-view mirror as the van pulls away. Reddish hair, sunken eyes. A Jew, no doubt. I'll remember you, friend, I think. The official waves me on without a glance, and I adjust my view of him. A loyal patriot.

Just as I'm about to put my foot down – another queue. Only then do I see the second border post. A woman in a chequered hat comes to my window. She speaks in English, so I hold up my passport, and she gives what I grudgingly accept is a winning smile, then asks – in perfect if accented Spanish – one of the most idiotic questions I have ever heard. 'Negocios o placer?' Pleasure? In Gibraltar?

Finally on the other side, I make it to ten kilometres an hour. To my left rises the Rock, cloud gathering around its peak, its sides pale and craggy, like the images I have in mind of the white cliffs of Dover. Albus, Albion, Perfidious Albion. I wonder what those dark holes are in the limestone. Caves? Tunnels? Dwelling places for the Gibraltarians? Suddenly I hit the brakes. A third queue and another police girl, hand raised.

Roadblock. Dios. I think of the compartment Hernán has hidden in the roof of the car. Ahead, a 'bobby' in a tit-head helmet is dragging a chain of spikes across the road. I twist on the fan, contemplating my options.

This fan is loud. *I turn it down but the roar continues, growing to a crescendo as ... An aeroplane has just landed ten metres in front of the bonnet of my car. A 747 jumbo, name splashed in gaudy orange on the fuselage, wheels screeching as the third-rate pilot struggles to bring it to a halt. Airport terminal. Control tower. Baggage handlers. The road into Gibraltar is bisected by a runway.* De puta madre!

The spikes are withdrawn, and at last I drive across the tarmac apron, flanked by moronic workers on pushbikes and aggressive youths on mopeds. Concrete council estates sprout on the other side, the narrow pavements jammed with cars. A red British phone box throbs on the street corner. Behind, filling my mirrors, is a London-style double-decker bus.

I turn left off the roundabout and pass a wholesaler's shop. The white van of earlier is parked outside. I memorise the name above the door, then press more deeply into the heart of the fortress.

Chapter Eighteen

The pile of reference books towered precariously at the edge of Spike's desk. He checked the time and found he'd been working for three hours straight. Only last week, anxiety about Zahra had been getting in the way of his work; now he realised that he'd barely had a chance to think of her in days. He felt a sudden stab of guilt as he imagined her abandoned in Italy, then remembered her cold impersonal voice on the phone, Jessica's insistence that she always found a way to come out of things on top. He would wait and see what Enrico Sanguinetti sent back from Portofino, then decide what to do next.

Back to the Merchant Shipping Act of 1894 . . . Something Clohessy had said about the cost of remaining moored in the Straits had suggested a possible line of attack. The competition Neptune faced from its rivals – you only had to type the company name into Google for the current location of their ship to come up – meant staying in possession of the site was all the more vital. The seas were full of unregulated salvage bandits, none of whom would be scrupulous enough to declare valuable unlisted cargo. Spike had found numerous examples of companies failing to disclose what they'd scavenged from the sea floor. Then there was the continuous harassment of the Guardia Civil: always worth bringing in the noisy Spanish neighbours to get a Gibraltarian court onside.

The one irritant was the lack of news from Jardine. A clear accord between the salvor and the Ministry of Defence was the starting point for the case. Friday lunchtime had come and gone without any contact. So much for military efficiency. Then, as if summoned, his desk phone rang. 'Spike Sanguinetti?'

'Hugh Jardine.'

'You're late.'

'Top brass took a while to debate. And we've decided not to press any claim on the silver.'

Spike paused. 'No claim at all?'

'Technically the silver bars are not MoD property.'

'I see.'

'You also said they would probably be confiscated by Customs and Excise.'

'It's possible.'

'And even if they aren't, well, frankly no one here can quite believe we're in for a multi-million payout for some old lead. We'd rather not rock the boat with Neptune, if you'll forgive the saying.'

'You do realise the value of the silver could be five times that of the lead?'

Jardine seemed to hesitate. 'Try and see it from our point of view, Spike. The MoD is suffering the most swingeing cuts since the end of the Cold War. There could be hundreds more ship-wrecks hidden in the Straits.' He chuckled. 'The wise man plays the long game.'

'So that's the official MoD position?'

'I'll have my secretary email through the documentation.'

'Very well. See you on Monday.'

'Monday?'

'The hearing.'

'I suppose I ought to be there.'

'I suppose you ought.'

Spike hung up. Baffling: Clohessy must have got to the MoD somehow. Discount the silver or we walk away. Ruthless bastard.

He returned to his skeleton argument, cross-checking it with Galliano's original notes. As he flicked through a printout detailing the scope of Gibraltar's territorial waters, he noticed a faint pencil mark in the margin he'd missed the first time round. He twisted the page, trying to decipher Galliano's sloping, artistic hand. 'Simon,' he read aloud, 'Grainger'. *Simon Grainger.* So Grainger really had been in touch with Galliano.

There was a phone number sketched beneath, which Spike dialled at once. '*Hola?*' came a female voice. A televisual hum in the background, then a peal of childish laughter. 'Is that Mrs Grainger?'

'Who is this?'

'Spike Sanguinetti.'

A long pause. 'I didn't give you this number.'

'That's what I'd like to see you about.'

Chapter Nineteen

Clinging to the slope above the land border with Spain was the Moorish Castle Estate, a cluster of medium-rise tower blocks rising from the ruins of the oldest part of Gibraltar, a fort built by the Arabs when they'd captured the Rock in AD 711. The castle's ancient stones intermingling with the cheap, post-war materials of government housing created a curious millennial clash of styles.

Spike stopped beneath the castle gatehouse. A family of apes were climbing down from the Upper Rock, using its creeper-clad wall as a bridge down into the estate. They moved in single file, two juveniles, a male, a stocky female up front – macaques were a matriarchal society, Spike remembered as he watched the mother turn and bare her fangs, then crouch for her mate to pick a flea from within her grey pelt. One of the juveniles vaulted across a gulf of a thousand years, clattering down onto a recycling bin shelter. It picked up a sun-bleached Walker's crisp packet, sniffed, then tossed it aside.

A brick-lined archway led towards the tower blocks. Macmillan House, Tankerville House . . . The nomenclature reminded Spike of cigarette brands: the cheaper the tobacco – Pall Mall, Regal – the grander the name. Patriotic graffiti – '*British Forever!*'; '*Give Spain No Hope*' – was scrawled on the retaining wall of a caged football ground, while the kerb was painted in red, white and blue, like a sun-drenched street in West Belfast. A woman in a velour tracksuit stood guard beside a boarded-up Social Club as a child urinated beneath the porch. 'Swings, Granny,' the girl demanded. *Granny?* She looked younger than Spike.

Spike gave the woman and child a nod, then passed beneath the Tower of Homage, the one part of the castle that was still intact. Not long ago it had housed Gibraltar's prison: there were tales of inmates escaping, cheerfully observed by residents, who would only grass them up if they had a Spanish look about them. The prison had since been moved to a purpose-built facility on the other side of the Rock; pigeons now nested in the battlements, though its air of incarceration remained, seeping somehow into the surrounding buildings.

Keightley House formed three sides of a square. Union Jacks and Gibraltar flags were draped from the upper windows, along with the inevitable selection of smalls and Liverpool FC beach towels. Pinned to one wall was a laminated notice from the Tenants Association. Apparently Gibraltar's Chief Minister was to visit next month to discuss 'widening the water mains'. '*Nob*', someone had scrawled helpfully by his name.

Spike pushed open the metal door to Block C. The pigeonholes were swollen with post – however grim the conditions, the fantastically low rent meant that government housing was always oversubscribed. Spike found the box marked 'Grainger' and wrestled out a wad of envelopes. Three were stamped 'On Her Majesty's Service', a misleadingly exciting phrase betokening income or council tax bills. A couple of stiff handwritten envelopes were addressed to 'Amy Grainger' – condolence cards, probably.

Flat 7B, the post-box said, so Spike started up the narrow staircase, apparently built for a generation of Gibraltarians expected to be short and undernourished. Two doors opened at the top of each flight, most with a cheap wall tile alongside, some offering welcome, others an image of a favoured saint – Bernard of Clairvaux, Patron Saint of Gibraltar; Our Lady of Fátima, a Portuguese madonna with a penchant for ghostly appearances.

An ironing board sat on the third floor, a man's designer white shirt stretched across it. The front door was of expensive oak; Spike had heard rumours of cigarette smugglers living on the estate in flats pimped out with marble bathrooms, jacuzzis, plasma TVs.

He paused on the sixth floor, slightly alarmed to find himself out of breath. The landing window appeared to be composed of jam-jar bases, a few panes missing, presumably to temper the heat. The view looked out onto the eastern face of the Rock, fourteen hundred feet of limestone cliff, O'Hara's Battery at the peak, a folly built by a former general to monitor the Spanish ships leaving Cádiz. Grainger must have stared at that view every day, Spike thought grimly, perhaps wondering how it might feel to jump.

A baby buggy lay folded outside the door to Flat 7B, its seat dotted with crumbs and stains. How anyone could drag it up here defied belief. Cheap rent or not, this was a cruel allocation for a young family. The welcome tile showed a country cottage with smoke furling from the chimney, 'God Bless Our Home' glazed above. Moved by the irony, Spike pushed in the stiff metal button of the doorbell, and waited.

Chapter Twenty

Footsteps, then a sliver of Mrs Grainger's pale face appeared in the doorway. A security chain jangled, and Spike was inside.

No cigarette smuggler's Aladdin's den for the Graingers, just two sagging brown sofas, so large that they must have been assembled in the flat, so old that the assemblers must be dead. The walls were laid with flock wallpaper, the TV of a similar vintage to Galliano's antique computer monitor. Spike had been wrong about the view: the kitchenette gave west, towards the Straits. Cranes jutted skywards from reclaimed land – luxury apartments for Category-II buyers, high-net-worth individuals whose only requirement to qualify for Gibraltar's tax rates was to own a property on the Rock 'appropriate to sustaining a wealthy lifestyle'. Whether they ever crossed the threshold was irrelevant.

'Sorry about the mess,' Amy Grainger said, pointing Spike towards the nearest sofa, 'I've been a little tired lately.' The sofa back was so high Spike failed to see the occupant until he'd almost crushed him: the little boy Charlie, lying on his stomach in a Spiderman vest and shorts, slotting shapes into a wooden cage. He peered up at Spike with eyes as solemn and dark as his mother's, then slid off the sofa onto a battered plastic pushcart, which he propelled over the wood-effect floor using just the tips of his bare feet.

'Your post,' Spike said, laying the envelopes on the coffee table.

The kettle was whistling. '*Tenkiù,*' Amy called back in *yanito*. 'Would you like a cup of tea?'

'Just some *agua de beber*, please.'

The kettle quietened down, and Amy reappeared with two china mugs of tap water. Charlie was sitting cross-legged by the kitchen table now. Spike realised he was shaking the shapes *out* of the box, an act of some dexterity.

Amy muted the cartoons on the television, then turned to Spike. 'How did you get my husband's number?'

He waited until she had sat down. She wore cut-off jogging pants and a stripy matelot top. A plastic hair clip held her black fringe to one side; she looked sad, and very young.

'It seems that Simon contacted my partner shortly before he died. His number was jotted down in a case file. Do you know why?'

'I told you, I found his business card in Simon's papers. I don't know why Simon met or even spoke to him.' From the kitchenette came the steady tick of wood against wood. Amy gave an embarrassed smile. 'I don't seem to know very much at all.'

Spike paused; he hated this part. 'Were you and your husband happy, Mrs Grainger?'

'What does that have to do with it?'

'Peter handles our divorce practice. I'm sorry, but I have to ask.'

She lowered her eyes. 'We were OK. Surviving. Like most people.'

'Why didn't you mention the toxicology report?'

Her voice fell. 'I don't understand.'

'The military pathologist concluded that your husband was taking prescription drugs.'

She didn't reply, so Spike pushed on: 'Did you know he was depressed, Mrs Grainger?'

Her lower lip began to tremble. 'A biscuit and your room,' she called to Charlie, who ran obediently to a cookie jar, removed a ginger nut and disappeared.

Spike passed her his handkerchief and waited. He was good at that at least – knew the power of a silence. Eventually she spoke. 'We met two years ago in Puerto Banús. I was on holiday with friends. Simon came from Falmouth, in Cornwall. Do you know it?'

'A little.'

'It was a holiday romance, I suppose. But he was interesting. Had opinions. What if Land's End was part of Spain, he used to say.' A smile played on her lips, then faded. 'When I found out I was pregnant, we decided to get married. My family would never have let me . . . you know. It just wasn't an option. We talked about moving to England but then the recession hit.' She reached for her water. 'It was all a bit of an adventure at first. Simon had been studying law in England; we thought he could continue here as a correspondence student. But when Charlie was born, it was all so expensive. He had to take a job at a restaurant in Ocean Village. When they gave him the role of manager, he accepted it. Things were tough but . . . I didn't know he was on antidepressants. He must have felt he couldn't tell me.' She was crying now, and Spike laid an awkward hand on her shoulder, cursing himself for getting involved. What had Peter been playing at with Simon Grainger? The widow nodded at the pile of envelopes, then forced herself to meet Spike's eye. 'I can't even pay the bills. Our account's stopped working. And my parents . . .' She lowered her head, and Spike took the opportunity to withdraw his hand on the pretext of examining the letters more closely. 'Simon's bank account has been frozen as part of probate. You need to settle your husband's estate. If you give me any outstanding bills, I can contact your bank and instruct them to switch the account into your name.'

Amy gave a small smile, and for a moment Spike could see the girl Grainger had met on a beach in Puerto Banús and hoped to take home to his mother. A classic Gibraltarian blend with her pale complexion and black hair – Maltese, Italian and Portuguese blood, no doubt spliced with the genes of a lustful British squaddie. 'You'd do that?' she said.

Spike nodded.

'And you'll keep looking into what happened to Simon?'

'I'll try,' he said, hastily gathering up the bills. 'Do you have any more of these?'

'In the bedroom.'

'Can you . . .' But she was already on her feet.

A police siren wailed from below. Estate kids probably, causing trouble. Spike looked back at the kitchenette and saw the little boy standing by the table, watching him. Spike smiled. Charlie didn't smile back.

Chapter Twenty-one

Walking away from Keightley House, relieved to be back in the sun, Spike saw an ambulance parked at the edge of the estate. He recognised one of the paramedics. 'Anything serious?'

The man pointed at a white van with two wheels mounted on the pavement. 'Hit the kerb,' he replied. 'Head into the steering wheel. That's why you wear a seatbelt.'

'Dead?'

'Extremely.'

'Gibraltarian?'

'One of the Benady brothers.'

'Alfie Benady?'

The paramedic's radio crackled into life; he nodded, then turned away to answer the call. Alfred Benady, Spike thought. Restaurant delivery driver. Four years above him at school. A couple of fist-fights with the SBS in the late Nineties, some drunk-and-disorderlies after his wife left him, two of them defended by Spike. Dead in his van after a minor prang. Not much of an obituary.

A dull-looking, bespectacled man in a blue car was rubber-necking the scene from the other side of the road. Spanish number plates: typical. Spike continued past him on foot towards Governor's Parade, keeping above Main Street, choosing a route that avoided the tourist hordes. Earlier he'd seen a cruise ship moored in the harbour: the passengers would be doing their rounds by now, cable car to the Upper Rock, St Michael's Cave, a few snaps of the apes, then back into town, stocking up on duty-free before moving on to Sardinia.

An email was waiting back at Chambers containing the MoD's official decision on the Neptune deal. Spike scrolled down, finding Jardine's instructions to his secretary at the base of the chain. 'Pls forward asap to counsel. Ta muchly, J'.

Poor woman, Spike thought as his mobile beeped. A new text: '8pm tonite at the Calpe? J xx'. J for Jardine, J for Jessica . . . Tossing his phone onto the desk, he took out Amy Grainger's sheaf of bills. Standard utilities, nothing too alarming. The most interesting piece of correspondence was an invoice from a workshop in Cádiz. *Monies to be paid on collection of goods.* Spike jotted down the address, then hit print on his skeleton argument, waiting impatiently as the sheets disgorged slowly from the mouth of the machine.

*

At last I find a space and swing the SEAT inside. The meter is demanding pound coins. Spanish is one of the most widely spoken languages in the world – second only to Mandarin. Yet on this ugly piece of Rock we are forced to put up with incestuous, six-fingered freeloaders calling themselves natives and talking in English. I know my history – all Spanish schoolchildren do. Gibraltar was forcibly stolen from Spain in 1704. The British claim it was ceded by the Treaty of Utrecht in 1713, but even they will admit that the terms were invalid, signed under duress. In any case, the Treaty provides that if Britain ever relinquishes sovereignty of the Rock, Spain has first refusal. Yet what did I drive past on the way here? A parliament building. Gibraltar has its own parliament, and if that isn't relinquishing sovereignty, I don't know what is. A dawn raid, I think to myself as I dig out three gold coins stamped with the head of the Queen of England and shove them into the machine. The Spanish navy, air force and army combined. It would all be over by breakfast.

He is still on the other side of the road. Tall and rangy, with a confident gait and a cool, thoughtful gaze. Looks like he could run fast if he had to. Thick dark hair cut short, face angular, high cheek-bones and a fine aquiline nose. Disconcerting eyes: bright blue, but set into a face which is naturally tan, darker now, I suspect, than at any other time of year, given the strength of the August sun when it chooses to break the cloud cover of this strange peninsula. Better-looking than the work-website photo Hernán gave me in the restaurant. When he pauses to greet someone, as he does quite often, he listens more than he speaks, weighing his words before answering, and when he smiles ... It feels hard-won, somehow, and I have seen his interlocutors shine long after he has let them go.

He stopped on the way here, as it happens, a few streets behind his office, to buy flowers, which interests me. He chose not the garish carnations and out-of-season roses that the local florists flog to tourists, but a small bunch of grape hyacinths, quietly lovely. He carries them at his side, careful with the stems, eyes moving occasionally to the sky, then the sea, then the buildings on either side, which he must have seen a thousand times but seems still to observe with interest.

One thing he doesn't see is me. I know that, because it's all I'm really watching out for. Then again, why would he, given how I'm dressed, the way I'm walking, the manner in which my hair and glasses are styled? You wouldn't. Who knows – perhaps you've missed me already.

He is passing business premises now, all of which are closed. The rest of Europe works itself to the bone in recession, while Gibraltar operates a 'Summer Hours' policy for July and August, offices open only between 10 a.m. and 2 p.m. He stops by a gleaming building that looks like it's been assembled from a flat-pack marked 'Crap Modern Architecture'. St Bernard's Hospital. Who but a Gibbo would name a hospital after a dog?

I'm about to cross the road when I see a bank of CCTV cameras ranged outside the entrance, so I sit down on the carpark wall of a supermarket of whose name I have never heard. I could have left the SEAT there for free.

Another grimy inbred is perching on the wall next to me. I slip a hand into my pocket and feel the comforting weight of the truncheon: retracted, it is no bigger than a flashlight. The man looks like a Romani, perhaps relegated from the scamming scene in Torremolinos. He unzips his bag to show off a handful of wooden bangles. My hand remains in my pocket, but I draw out a five-pound note and say, 'Two, please,' to which he shows his stumpy teeth, grabbing my English cash and passing me the bangles along with a tatty card emblazoned with a mountain and some kind of gypsy blessing.

I edge along the wall, taking out my pay-as-you-go phone, which attracts the man for a millisecond until he sees how cheap it is. Thank you, Hernán. His focus shifts to some shoppers coming out of this 'Morrisons', and already I can see I am forgotten.

I drop the bangles down a drain. When I look back up, my target is standing inside the hospital's reception area – a softly spoken line to the woman behind the desk, which produces another warm blush, and he's off again, walking back the way he came, face downcast. Worrying about someone, perhaps. I can work with that.

I follow him back towards the Old Town. The SEAT will have to wait, I realise, as he's going into a pub now, one of a hundred establishments that foul this place like pustules, reeking of stale beer and deep-fried food. The Royal Calpe. Another word I will have to look up back at the hotel.

I sit down on the pub terrace. 'Toilets For Customers Only', the sign on the window counsels. Really? The plastic tables are spattered in gulls' shit and cluttered with other people's filthy glasses. Behind the bar, the bottle-blonde waitress doesn't see me, let alone come out to take my order.

I watch him through the open doors. He's with a girl now –
predictable, you might say, except that I'd been starting to
wonder if he was a fag, given his pretty-boy face and naked ring
finger. He and the girl touch cheeks, and I can see she's keen, not
just from her flush, which I'm getting used to now, but from the
intensity of her gaze, as though she's afraid to let him out of her
sight. She's a good deal smaller than him, as are most of his
compatriots, but with large breasts for such a petite frame. Her
trim figure suggests she works out – a fitness instructor, maybe,
until I see her slip a paperback into her bag. He buys the drinks,
she watches, smiling up at him as he returns. Nice to find a tradi-
tional girl on this Rock.

I take out a book of my own, but I can't seem to read anything
of substance in this place, the heat and humidity are too high. I
find myself thinking of the hotel room I must return to tonight,
an overpriced broom cupboard in a converted barracks. The din
of cheap talk shows drifting up from the lobby TV. The shared
bathroom. The fire-drill on the back of the door, in English and
pidgin Spanish, the latter corrected in felt-tip pen by an angry
previous guest.

Hunger stirs, but there's nothing to eat here but fish-n-chips
and all-day English breakfasts. Earlier I saw a restaurant named
'TAPS'. I assumed this was tapas, misspelt, but no – an array of
warm beers. I ended up buying some ham and chips from a
Moroccan speaking in English, his congealed offering wrapped in
a Spanish newspaper.

A deep loathing for Hernán starts to fill my gorge. Why can't I
just do the job and leave? Why does he have to make things so . . .
complicated?

My target is coming out again – he and the girl walk directly
past me, parting outside the Cathedral, her lips lingering a little
too long on his cheek. 'See you tomorrow,' she calls after him.
She's still standing there, watching, as I fall in behind him, but she
doesn't see me, not even a glance.

Barbers and beauty parlours are doing a brisk trade in the Old Town. He walks past them, a slight spring in his step, as though he actually likes these damp narrow alleyways and high-walled passages. The crowds are thinning, and I realise now that I must take care. I let him get ahead, then consult the web of streets in my mind which yesterday's wanderings have already imprinted. I rejoin him on Castle Road; he's hesitant now, as if he can sense something. He glances back, but I am too quick for him, stepping behind one of the red phone boxes that exist even at the top of this ancient anthill. When I find him again he looks more relaxed, perhaps rebuking himself for his earlier paranoia.

He enters a dingy alley and I linger on the corner, beneath a birdcage attached to a first-floor balcony. The budgerigar peers down at my face, then tucks its head behind a wing. He stops again. The ground-floor lights are on; he raises his fists, and for a moment I think he is going to spin round, that he's seen me, but no . . . he is raging at the night sky, lambasting some unseen deity. I could almost grow to like this man.

As soon as he's inside the house, I circumvent the alley and re-enter at the other end. Through the kitchen window, I see him lit up, talking to a stick man with white hair and a quarrelsome brow. I reach into my pocket, feeling the smooth form of the truncheon. Patience, I think. Patience.

Chapter Twenty-two

Spike had assumed that Jessica would want to talk on the bus journey, but in fact she'd slept throughout, head occasionally lolling onto his shoulder. They'd met as planned on Winston Churchill Avenue at 9 a.m., crossing the land border on foot to the Spanish town adjacent to Gib, La Línea de la Concepción, avoiding the vehicle queues already forming. As soon as they'd boarded the bus for Cádiz, Jessica had tipped back the seat and closed her eyes.

As the bus rattled through the coastal towns of Andalucía – Tarifa, Bolonia, San Fernando – Spike found himself thinking back to similar journeys he'd made with Zahra. The time in Malta they'd visited Gozo, travelling the length of the island to reach Ċirkewwa harbour, Zahra's quiet excitement as she'd shown him the landmarks she had already discovered during her short stay. Their desert trip in Morocco, when they'd first fallen for each other. Why the hell had she called him, he wondered again. If she'd really moved on, and no longer cared, why bother making contact at all?

He glanced down and saw that Jessica had left a drool-mark on the shoulder of his T-shirt. Out of the window, a first bull silhouette appeared on the brow of a hill – four tonnes of black steel advertising a brand of Spanish brandy. The figures had become an unofficial symbol of Spain, ignoring the fact that the company responsible for them had been founded by a Brit, one Thomas Osborne Mann, an eager young trader from Exeter who'd settled in Cádiz in the late eighteenth century.

The rhythm of the engine settled as the bus entered Cádiz's suburbs, and Jessica opened her eyes. '*Manascada*,' she yawned. 'How much did we have to drink last night?'

Spike could sense the Spaniard in the seat behind bristle at the sound of her soft *yanito*. He remembered the last time he'd been to Cádiz, on a school trip, when they'd been studying the Singeing of the King of Spain's Beard in class. The land border between Spain and Gib – closed by General Franco for fourteen years – had just been reopened as a condition of Britain allowing Spain to join the EU. 'Whatever you do, speak Spanish,' their History teacher had told them nervously on the coach. 'It's *Caddy*, not Cádiz. I don't want to hear any "z"s . . .'

'*Por bashe*,' Spike replied now to Jessica, enjoying a childish thrill at no longer being in the thrall of school authorities.

The bus stopped at Plaza de la Hispanidad, and Spike and Jessica got off. The journey had only lasted an hour and a quarter, quicker than he'd remembered.

'What time's your appointment?' Jessica asked.

'Not for another hour.'

They took a brief stroll around the square. Spike had forgotten how pretty Cádiz was – built on a peninsula like Gib, but with white eighteenth-century townhouses fashioned from the limestone rather than functional military properties.

'I don't think I've been here since we were at school,' Jessica said.

'Were you on that trip?'

'We sat next to each other on the way back. Don't you remember?' She smoothed her dark hair into a ponytail, averting her eyes.

'I remember the beach,' Spike said. 'We weren't allowed on it.'

'We could see it now? It's never too late for breakfast.'

Leaving the square, they strolled south towards the seafront, passing the ornate facade of the Gran Teatro Falla, taking in the street names honouring heroes of Spanish literature – Calle de Cervantes, de Calderón de La Barca.

'Wow,' Jessica murmured as the avenue opened into the Playa de La Caleta, wider and more golden than any beach in Gib. Breakers smashed in the surf; Cádiz lay to the west of Gibraltar so its shoreline was unbroken Atlantic. 'Not so good for swimming,' Spike countered as they stepped off the pavement onto the sand. His need to defend Gib was hardwired.

A kiosk was selling freshly grilled sardines; Spike bought a paper plate for them both and carried them down to the waterfront.

'Next stop the New World,' Jessica said, sitting down on the sand and fizzing open a can of Diet Coke. Spike took in the sea forts framing the beach. At least Gib had the edge there, he decided as he sat down next to her and stared at the gleaming expanse of ocean.

Time passed; Spike checked his phone as Jessica picked the meat off a sardine with a plastic fork. Spike slipped the entire fish into his mouth and drew out the forked tail. Jessica smiled as he sucked in air over his palate.

'It's hot,' he tried to say.

'It's what?' she laughed.

He shook his head and swallowed, relishing the strong flavour of the red-brown meat. Fresh sardine was good, the tinned variety the poorest of substitutes. Unlike tuna, which Spike secretly preferred in its metal coffin. 'So,' he said. 'Hamish.'

Jessica tightened her ponytail and looked stubbornly out to sea. 'What about him?'

'Are you still in touch?'

'He emails.' She paused: 'I don't.'

Spike busied himself with another fish, unsure whether to press her further. 'Are you considering . . .'

'Forgiving him? No, Spike, I'm not.' She turned aggressively. 'What kind of shit cheats on his fiancée the night before their wedding?'

'Perhaps I shouldn't have mentioned it to you.'

She gave a wry smile. 'Well, it's a bit late now, isn't it? Anyway, what about Zahra? Any news?'

'I'm following your advice.'

'That's a first. Which bit?'

'Concentrating on the future.'

'So you're not planning to keep looking?'

Spike shrugged, placing a hand on the sand and squeezing his fingers through the warm grains.

'But you must miss her, I mean . . .'

'OK,' Spike said. 'Let's cut a deal. I won't mention Hamish if you don't ask about Zahra. What do you say?'

She nodded, and they shook hands, hers hot and clammy. Hungover or embarrassed. A bit of both, probably.

He ate another sardine, trying to mask the hollow feeling which had returned to his stomach, the questions that wouldn't go away. What if Jessica was wrong about Zahra? If she was still in trouble? If Peter really had been attacked because of him?

'Shall we?' Spike asked, suddenly keen to leave.

'One moment more,' Jessica said, lying back. 'I love the sound of the Atlantic.'

Reluctantly, Spike lay down beside her, pushing his mind back to the summer after A-levels, the glorious empty months before he'd taken up his Gibraltar Government Scholarship and moved to London to read Law at UCL. He'd felt part of a crowd then – Jessica, Sebastian Alvarez . . . Others too, but he couldn't remember them clearly. Most evenings they'd walked to Eastern Beach, the best stretch of sand Gib had to offer. Built bonfires, played volleyball, drunk spirits from the bottle as the sun set over the Straits. It was after one of those nights that Spike had come home to find his father sitting in the kitchen. No sign of his mother. 'She's gone, son,' Rufus had whispered, and Spike had assumed she'd left – he wouldn't have blamed her. But no, he hadn't meant that at all.

'You OK?' Jessica said, sitting up.

'*Grevi.*' He sprang athletically to his feet, then felt dizzy, so dropped to his knees, ostensibly to pick up the remains of their lunch.

'I love the way you never leave any trace of yourself. Like a cat.'

'Really?' Spike said. 'What an odd thing to admire.'

A group of noisy teenagers was strolling down the beach, girls in string bikinis, boys punting a football as though expecting to be scouted by FC Barcelona. They passed Spike and Jessica without a glance, then sprinted into the surf.

From the road, a middle-aged man was watching, leaning against a blue car. For a second Spike thought he was staring at Jessica, but then his gaze switched to the teenagers as they ducked in and out of the water, squealing.

Chapter Twenty-three

Spike and Jessica returned to the centre of Cádiz via Calle Sagasta. What Spike had remembered as a thriving commercial street was now lined by boarded-up shops and pawnbrokers. He was used to La Línea being rundown – people even said that the Spanish government kept it that way as a punishment for Gib – but the great Cádiz? The oldest city in western Europe? Suddenly Spike could see how the Spanish must feel as they read about the Rock's booming economy, saw its new buildings, heard its jumbo jets, learnt of the only government in Europe that earned more than it spent. Not just British, but openly defying the economic downturn through low taxation. He passed a posse of Spanish students smoking dope on a park bench. Thank God for twenty-first-century apathy: the next Spanish siege was still some way off.

'I think that's the Archaeological Museum,' Jessica said, pointing to a townhouse resting in the shade of a mimosa tree. Behind it spread a more modern residential area of pale-cement apartment blocks. Spike reread the address on the bill, then rang a buzzer. A man's tenor voice answered. '*Sí?*'

'*Hablamos por teléfono,*' Spike replied, wincing at how rusty his Spanish accent was becoming.

'You are Simon's friend from Gibraltar,' the voice said, switching to a serviceable English. 'Where is he? Why has he sent you?'

'*Es muerto.*' Muerto ... There was so much more life to the Spanish word than its velvet-covered English equivalent, Spike thought as he heard a breath catch at the end of the line. 'You have the money?'

'Six hundred euros.'

The door gave a click. Jessica glanced at Spike and raised an eyebrow. He grinned and pushed into the apartment hallway.

The lift opened to a grey-haired couple carrying a picnic hamper and a yellow parasol. They nodded at Spike and Jessica, sharing a wistful smile as they shuffled out together onto the street. Spike guided Jessica into the lift, then hit floor three.

A boy was waiting outside the lift doors. Crossed arms, black-rimmed glasses, heavy-metal T-shirt. On closer examination, not a boy, but an unfortunately short twenty-something. He glanced from Spike to Jessica, then blushed so fiercely that the shaving rash on his neck was visible. 'This way,' he said, tossing his tousled black hair to one side. Why not, thought Spike – the flash of scalp suggested that he would not be tossing it for long.

The apartment was surprisingly stylish, walls decorated with architectural *vedute* and oils of Moorish streets. A paella dish sat on the stove, Miele dishwasher sloshing beneath. Parents' place, Spike decided uncharitably, remembering the youth's unabashed admiration of Jessica.

The study off the kitchen overlooked a yellow-grassed communal garden. A sleek olivewood desk was covered with architectural plans and elevations, while the far end of the room had been given over to some sort of workshop, a plastic table cluttered with solvents and paints, a laptop on the floor surrounded by computer-game sleeves.

Jessica glanced at a framed diploma propped against the wall. 'Archaeological Honours,' she read aloud. 'Juan Andrés Gonzalez. That's you, right?'

'Who else would it be?' Juan lifted a small metal cashbox onto the table. 'Money, please,' he said to Spike.

'I'd like to see what we're buying first.'

Juan pulled a wooden crate from beneath the desk. Drawing out some balled newspaper, he carefully removed what looked like a Roman helmet and placed it on the table. The object was small, no more than fifty centimetres high and made of a blue-black metal, its surface covered in greenish growths, as though lugworms had burrowed inside. Spike leant down to take a closer look. 'What *is* it?'

Juan stared at him, as though suddenly realising he was talking to someone of subnormal intelligence. 'It's a ship's bell, *señor*,' he said. 'Simon brought it to me to be restored.' He switched his gaze from one blank face to the other. 'I'm a conservator?' he said, intonation suggesting he feared they might not understand the word.

'So you work at the museum,' Jessica replied.

Juan pushed his hair back defensively. 'Their funding got cut. But I still do some private work. Now please, the money.'

Spike held out the envelope, then withdrew it. 'Doesn't look like you've done much by way of restoration.'

'The bell has bronze disease. There was nothing that could be done.'

Spike examined a bottle of white vinegar on the table. 'Clearly a high-end job.'

'I hadn't realised you were an expert in metallurgy.'

'Did you do much work for Simon?'

'You a cop or something?'

Jessica stepped between them. She stood almost at Juan's height. 'We're friends of Simon's wife,' she smiled reassuringly. 'We're just helping her to sort out his estate, OK?' She extracted the envelope from Spike's grip and handed it to Juan. He opened it, fingering the sides of the notes. 'Simon brought me a number of pieces,' he said more equably. 'He wanted them cleaned so he could sell them on.'

'Just cleaned?' Spike said, turning over a pile of papers on the table and finding sheets of museum headed paper.

'And identified.'

'Items the museum wouldn't touch.'

Juan gave a non-committal shrug.

'Why didn't Simon get the work done in Gibraltar?'

'Most of the objects came from the sea, and in Gibraltar, you need to surrender whatever you find. But bring something into Spain, and if it's from Gibraltar, who cares?' He glanced at Spike's expression. 'The first time, Simon brought me a flagon of gin. Then a manila bracelet – handcuffs used for transporting slaves.' Jessica frowned, so he moved on rapidly. 'Then an eighteenth-century ship's bell.'

'It's that old?' Spike said.

'You can tell from the size. It might have been quite valuable. If it didn't have bronze disease.'

'What *is* bronze disease?'

Juan looked down and brushed a thumb over the blue growths protruding from the surface of the bell. 'An irreversible corrosion of the metal. Archaeologists used to think the deterioration was caused by bacteria. Now they know it's the result of a chemical reaction, like rust on iron-based metals. Simon should have put it in a bucket of salty water the moment he brought it out of the sea.'

'So it's worthless.'

'Depends on how much you're into eighteenth-century ships' bells. I've cleaned off most of the tarnish with a scalpel. You can still make out a few letters of the inscription. There are some so-so carvings on the rim.' He put the envelope into the cashbox and locked it. 'Simon told me he was going to give it to his wife.' He dropped the key into the pocket of his baggy jeans, then peered up, a concerned look suddenly crossing his chubby face. 'How did Simon die?' he asked.

'He killed himself.'

'Oh.' As if losing interest, Juan checked his watch. 'I have to go. You guys should probably . . .' His voice tailed off as he picked up the bell and slipped it back into the crate.

'Anything else belonging to Simon in here?' Spike said.

Juan shook his head. 'He sold whatever I restored. I think he had a buyer in Marbella.'

Jessica touched Spike's shoulder. 'Come on.'

'Sign this,' Spike said, taking out the invoice.

'I never had to sign anything before.'

'Well you do now.'

Grabbing a Mont Blanc pen from a holder on Juan's father's desk, Spike pressed it into his son's hand. Then he took back the receipt, picked up the crate and followed Jessica out of the flat.

Chapter Twenty-four

They stepped back onto the street. The sun had risen above Cádiz and Spike's eyes ached in the glare. He envied Jessica her over-sized Gucci sunglasses.

'Jesus,' she said. 'You're so *aggressive*.'

'Sorry?'

'I thought you were going to smack him.'

'He was a scumbag.'

'He was a *kid*.'

Spike held up the crate: 'Six hundred euros for this?' On one side was written *Fino Quinta Osborne*. 'The box is worth more. His parents have taste, at least.'

Jessica set off down the street towards the bus station. 'You never used to be like this,' she called back to him.

'Like what?'

'Using your size to intimidate people. What's your problem?'

Spike mulled the question as they came into the Plaza de España, stopping in front of a white monument built to celebrate some long-abandoned Spanish constitution. 'I suppose I don't like people abusing their position,' he said.

'He was broke.'

'Taking money from a widow and child?'

Jessica swung round to face him. 'Please don't tell me you have a thing for this Grainger woman.'

'She's a client.'

'An extremely pretty client. That's why the *Chronicle* wasted so much copy on her.' Jessica walked on at pace, then called over one shoulder, 'Jesus, Spike. She's about fifteen!'

Spike had to run to catch her up. It took him ten minutes to calm her down. Then another five to persuade her to have a drink with him.

Chapter Twenty-five

Four *finos* later, it was Spike who slept on the bus home. As he woke they were coming into Algeciras, Gibraltar's opposing port on the Spanish side of the bay. A line of striped, barber's-pole chimneystacks flanked one side of the road. Franco had built a petrochemical plant near the town in the hope that it would belch fumes into Gibraltar's face. Unfortunately, the planners had failed to calculate the contrary winds of the Straits, and the pollution had blown inwards, blighting the area with one of the highest rates of bowel cancer in Spain.

Spike looked round and saw Jessica staring at him, sipping from a can of San Pellegrino orangeade. 'You look like a little boy when you sleep.' Unsure how to respond to this, he took the can from her grasp and drank deeply, tasting the salt from her mouth on the rim.

'I meant to ask,' she said. 'How's Peter?'

Spike sat up. Outside, the sun was setting. 'He's having a CAT scan on Tuesday, then I'm meeting his sister. There's going to be a formal discussion with the doctors.'

'*Cacarucca*,' Jessica murmured. 'Is there anyone else? In his life, I mean.'

'I'm not sure. We never really talked about that stuff.'

'He goes to Corfu, doesn't he? In the summer?'

'I know he inherited a house there. He's been meaning to do it up for years.'

The bus stopped to let off the Algeciras passengers. Now it was just Gibraltarians and *Linenses*, residents of La Línea. The usual quiet analysis of who was who rippled through the bus.

'How did you first meet Peter?' Jessica asked.

'He was at Ruggles & Mistry when I joined the firm. Fifteen years ago, maybe.'

'What was he like then?'

'The same. Just fatter.' Spike smiled. 'You know what Ruggles lawyers are like. Machines. Well, Peter was different. He liked wine, flamenco, Laurel and Hardy. Random things. You could smoke in the office in those days. We used to share a room – wave at each other through the fug.'

Jessica laughed. 'I forgot you used to smoke.'

'The partners would come in and weep.'

'Was that why he got made redundant?'

'For smoking?' Spike heard the mockery in his tone and hated himself for it. 'Technically Peter wasn't made redundant. They just failed to promote him, year after year. One day he told me he was leaving. Took me out for a boozy lunch and asked me to come in with him. So I forfeited my bonus. And off we went.'

'Bit of a risk.'

'Not with Peter. He always had his own clients. A collection of oddballs Ruggles couldn't be bothered with, but who were strangely lucrative if you weren't too fussy and would put in the time.'

'And the rest is history.'

The finality of the phrase troubled Spike. 'Aren't you going to hand that in?' Jessica asked, gesturing at the crate as they got off the bus at the Gibraltar frontier.

'Or what, Detective Sergeant Navarro?'

She grinned.

'Let me put it this way,' Spike said as they approached the first set of customs, 'if somebody confiscates it, I'll live.'

Chapter Twenty-six

'Thank the Lord,' Spike muttered as they neared the house. The kitchen lights were out. 'Dad's taken to staying up late to finish the crossword.'

'What happened to the watercolours?'

'Gone. He's onto the next thing.'

Jessica swayed a little in the alleyway. They'd stopped by the Royal Calpe on the way home. The neighbours' budgie stared down with accusatory black eyes as Spike unlocked the door, chattering sociably as Jessica raised a finger to the bars of the cage. 'Aren't you ever tempted to set it free?'

'During the day there are queues of other birds trying to get in. Isn't that what they say about marriage?' He held open the front door, realising that he'd been half-expecting Zahra to be standing behind him. They'd had many such evenings.

'My parents have been happily married for almost forty years,' Jessica retorted.

They walked into the kitchen, and suddenly Spike saw it through Jessica's eyes. Blister packs of his father's pills on the windowsill. Net of sprouting onions on top of the fridge. Redundant dog basket full of newspapers.

'Has your father been collecting ships' bells as well?' Jessica said, gesturing at the tea chests by the fridge.

Spike slipped the charred foil carton of an M&S steak-and-ale pie into the bin, then set down his own crate on the table. 'Nothing would surprise me. Drink?'

'Thought that was a no-no chez Sanguinetti.'

'You just have to know where to look.'

Spike reached to the top of the kitchen units and took down a bottle of J&B. He'd got a taste for the stuff in Tangiers. 'Don't worry,' he said, seeing Jessica's frown. 'I just keep it in reserve for guests.' He poured out two large amber slugs, knowing what she must be thinking. Boozy mum, boozy son. 'To our moratorium.'

'Sorry?'

'Our agreement not to talk about Zahra and Hamish.'

Zahra would have known what 'moratorium' meant, Spike thought as Jessica raised her glass. '*Heri hof*,' she toasted cheerily.

He watched from beside the table as she walked across the kitchen. Her dark hair was loose now, damp from the humidity and alcohol. The top button of her blouse had come undone, her skin browner than usual from the Cádiz sun, revealing the swell of her breasts, famous since their schooldays. She stooped to General Ironside's basket and fingered the worn tartan material. 'Why don't you get him another dog?'

'If you see any Jack Russells for sale in Gib, be sure to let me know.' Spike looked away, removed the ship's bell from the box, then sat down.

'How is your Dad these days?' Jessica said.

'Not too bad, actually. He's slowed down a bit since last year. Though he's getting obsessed with the past, which is slightly . . .' Spike trailed off. The design around the rim of the bell was really rather beautiful. A band of fleurs-de-lys, punctuated by a crown motif. Words were engraved around the top: most of the letters were cankered beyond recognition, but two or three remained legible. He reached for the kitchen pad.

'What are you doing, Spike?'

'You can still make out a few of the letters. I'm trying to work out the rest.'

'Does it matter?'

'The bell might be worth more if Amy decides to sell it.'

'Amy?'

'Mrs Grainger.'

'Enough whisky for you there?'

Spike realised he'd poured himself another glass. He drained it and said nothing as Jessica hovered at his shoulder. 'I just think you should watch yourself,' she said quietly. 'With the booze.'

He set down his pen and rubbed his eyes with both hands. 'Do you really?' He suddenly felt tired: bone-weary and ready for a fight. 'And when do I ever tell you what to do?'

'Maybe you would if you cared more.'

'Oh, spare me this tonight, Jess.'

She looked as though she was going to say something, but instead turned and pushed through the bead curtain. He heard the front door close quietly behind her – even now she was thinking of Rufus's sleep. He knew she wanted him to go after her, but somehow he didn't have the energy. Tomorrow they would talk it over. Laugh it off, as they always did.

It was properly dark outside now. As he closed the curtains, he thought he glimpsed a figure move by the window, then saw it was just the shadows cast by the washing line, waving in the levanter. He suddenly felt trapped, suffocated by the close air. He checked the time. 9 p.m., still early. So he downed his whisky, then boxed up the ship's bell and went out onto the street.

*

The management has provided no dressing gown, ergo it is my privilege to pace the upper corridors of this hotel clad only in a towel. A plastic mop-bucket sits by the bathroom door, forgotten by the cleaner or simply abandoned. I lock myself in the privy, gagging at the chip fat and fag smoke seeping up through the ventilation system, mingling with the shit-stench of the last occupant. Laughter drifts up as well: the downstairs television is onto the evening comedy slate now, the roster of British talk shows and soap operas over. Idiot me: as if there were going to be complimentary toiletries in here. Just a soap dispenser marked Kimberly Clark, whoever she may be. Empty, of course. I poke a finger into the spout and emerge with a single spot of soap. That's it – that's all I have to work with. I wait for the shower to dampen my freshly cut hair, then root my fingertip around the crevices of my body.

'Evenin',' smiles a fellow guest as I walk back to my room, an elderly skinhead with faded blue tattoos on his arms. I unlock my door and climb into bed to dry off, as my scrap of towel refuses to absorb moisture. To block out the monkey-shrieks from downstairs, I plug my travel speakers into my laptop and click on some classical guitar, feeling the soft cow-gut strings of Rodrigo, my namesake, start to balm my mind.

As I stretch out, I think back to the smug face of the Yid van driver, his unfettered shock as I reared up at his open window as he was having his lunch, the precision of my single blow to the forehead, the indentation perfectly aligned with the top rung of the steering wheel. A dip to the handbrake, a step back as the van mounted the pavement. Twenty-two seconds, all in. Are you sure you're still up to it . . . ?

The guitar sings on, and I glance at the bedside table. Beneath the toadstool-shaped plastic lamp, my mobile phone is winking. 'New plan,' the message says. 'Additional item to collect'. Well, I think as I switch off the music and pull another white polo shirt over my head, at least we're getting somewhere.

Chapter Twenty-seven

Spike took the steps of Upper Castle Gully three at a time. Still this odd sensation of being followed. When he reached the corner of Calpe Road, he stopped sharply and glanced over one shoulder. The moonlight reflected off the front of an abandoned video-rental shop. A thorn bush had seeded itself inside the doorway. Beyond, the lights of the Straits flickered with the usual night-time shipping.

He was about to press on when he heard a twig snap. Carefully, he put down his crate, feeling a drop of sweat slide down his forehead, blurring his vision. Wiping his eye, he kicked at the branches in front. A rustle of foliage as a small, grey-furred arm extended. A couple of footholds, and a sleepy young ape appeared, climbing onto the windowsill above, glaring down with what looked like tremendous irritation.

Spike felt his tension drain away as the ape scrutinised him, its jutting brow and intelligent green eyes disturbingly human. Marked on its underside was a faded tattoo – each of the apes was numbered by the wardens of the Upper Rock, mirroring the skin-art of many of the tourists who visited them. Zahra had told him that there were still tribes in Morocco and Algeria for whom Barbary macaques were 'commensals', living as equals, sharing the same table. The penalty for killing them was death. These days, in Gib, you'd probably be awarded the keys to the city. Churchill had famously said that Britain would lose the Rock if the apes ever left. With an endless supply of tourist snacks to tempt them, sovereignty seemed assured.

As Spike watched the monkey stalk grumpily away into the shadows, he remembered an occasion when he'd seen one steal a sandwich from a bemused backpacker – the ape had parted the bread, thrown out the ham, then tucked in. 'They are Muslims,' the tour guide had said with a smile. 'Remember where they came from.'

Back on Castle Road, Spike suppressed a shiver as he thought of the articles he'd browsed online about Simon Grainger's death. It seemed that though the apes had refrained from eating the body, they'd enjoyed toying with it, even tearing off an arm smashed by the fall.

The first tower of the Moorish Castle Estate appeared, its windows dark but for the occasional blue glow of a TV behind net curtains. Spike glanced down at the crate in his arms and considered turning back. Then he imagined how dispiriting it would be to return to his father's empty kitchen and its unsettling heap of tea chests. Two dirty glasses and nothing but a bottle of J&B to obliterate the rest of the night.

The door on the seventh floor opened cautiously. 'Who is it?'

'Spike Sanguinetti.'

The crack widened and he saw Amy Grainger looking up at him. With her wet black hair scraped back, and her face naked of make-up, she looked incredibly young.

Spike suddenly felt drunk and stupid. 'I brought you something.'

'I've only just got Charlie down.'

'From where?'

'To sleep.'

'Oh. Sorry.' He'd forgotten about the boy. She looked down at the crate. 'You'd better come in then.'

He followed her inside. As if trying to reclaim her own space, she'd cleared away most of the childish things and dimmed the lights. A pot on the stove smelled of tomato *ragù*; Spike wondered if she'd been expecting someone, then saw the single plate and glass on the table.

'It's been hard to get him to sleep lately,' she said, turning off the hob.

'I know the feeling,' Spike said, but she didn't smile back, perhaps taking in his crumpled T-shirt, the whisky on his breath. He realised with a sting of shame that she might be scared of him. 'Listen, I won't stay. I just wanted to give you this.' He passed her the box. 'I went to Cádiz today to settle the final bill.'

'This is what the six hundred euro invoice was for?'

Spike nodded as she drew out the contents. 'Simon was having it restored for you. It's a ship's bell,' he added sheepishly, guessing it might well be the worst present she had ever received.

'What was Simon *thinking* . . .' she said, running a finger over the blistered metal. She wrinkled her nose. 'God, it smells.'

'That's vinegar. Juan tried to clean it.'

'Juan?'

'The conservator in Cádiz. Apparently Simon had a line selling artefacts to tourist shops in Marbella. Juan helped get them into saleable condition.'

Amy stared at him. She looked good without make-up. Softer somehow.

'Did you know about it?'

She smiled. 'Come with me.'

He followed her through the kitchenette, peering over her shoulder as she opened a utility cupboard. On the shelves lay a medley of items: a shiny pink conch, a clay pipe, two ancient bulb-shaped bottles. 'Simon's trophy cabinet,' she said. 'He used to dive the Europa Reef with his friends from the restaurant. They would bring things back that got caught on the coral.'

'Expensive hobby.'

'What?'

'Diving.'

'He took his PADI course in Thailand. The staff from the restaurant were allowed to borrow stuff for free from the dive shop next door.'

Squatting on the central shelf was a coil of ship's rope. On top of it lay a rusty disc. 'Is that a coin?' Spike said, peering in further.

'A piece of eight, apparently.'

She picked up the coin and handed it to Spike. Medallion-sized, but light as a seashell, the metal flaking with the same blue-green contusions as he had seen on the bell. Bronze disease, no doubt, Spike thought as he handed it back. Amy bent down and placed the bell carefully on the bottom shelf, then closed the cupboard. 'You shouldn't have paid all that money,' she said as she stood back up, finding herself closer to Spike than she'd perhaps intended.

'You can pay me back. Anyway, I've sent the documentation to the bank. Your account should be working by Wednesday.'

'You've been so kind.'

He turned for the door.

'Let me at least give you supper,' Amy called after.

He hesitated. 'Are you sure you have enough?'

'It's pasta, for God's sake.'

Releasing the door handle, he stepped back into the room.

Chapter Twenty-eight

'So you were at the Sacred Heart Middle School?'

Amy started to sing: '*We are so proud/ To be part of this crowd/ In this sacred school of ours. This heart on a mount/ Where we all spell and count/ And we spend such happy hours . . .*'

'OK,' Spike said, raising a hand in supplication. 'I believe you.'

She smiled. 'My family used to live on Flat Bastion Road.'

'What's your maiden name?'

'Divinagracia . . . Amy Elizabeth Divinagracia.'

'As in Aiden Divinagracia?'

'You've met my brother, then.'

Spike shrugged, embarrassed to have brought up the connection. 'It's not an easy surname to forget.'

'In the Juvenile Court, right?'

Spike thought back to the short, anaemic shoplifter he had prosecuted twice. On the second occasion, he'd been waiting for Spike behind the Law Courts, threatening him with a flick-knife before realising that Spike had survived the same playgrounds, knew the same tricks. There were no private schools in Gibraltar, so future politicians, lawyers and criminals all studied together in the same classrooms.

'He's in Fuengirola now. We don't talk about him much these days.'

Spike busied himself with his tagliatelle. The tomato sauce was sweet and delicious. 'I wouldn't have had you down as a Divinagracia,' he said, failing to come up with any other topic of conversation.

'Because of my accent? I had to tone it down or Simon couldn't understand me. *Keki* or *gingibier*?' she asked, switching to a thick Gibraltarian.

Spike smiled. 'I'm OK with the wine, thanks.'

She picked up the box and topped up his glass. 'We were all terrified of your father at school.'

'His bark is worse than his bite.'

'You should have seen some of the female teachers. They used to swoon over Mr Sanguinetti.'

'Please,' Spike said, feeling slightly nauseous.

'I think it was his height. And the blue eyes . . .' She tilted her head, watching him sideways through her dark eyelashes.

'Northern Italian blood, allegedly,' Spike said. 'Foothills of the Alps.'

There was a silence. 'Have you ever been married?' she asked.

'No.'

'Close?'

'I've had a bad run of it.'

'Tell me about it, *compa*.' Amy peered down at her still-shiny wedding ring. Her small hands had long fingers, nails bitten as short as a schoolgirl's. The monitor gave a sudden whimper, green lights flashing.

'Is he waking up?' Spike said.

'Just a bad dream.' She got to her feet. 'He'll be OK as long as Bugs is with him.'

'Bugs?'

'His rabbit.' Amy moved to the sideboard where an old vinyl record player sat beneath an anglepoise lamp.

'Did Simon dig that out of the bay as well?'

She laughed, then held up the sleeve of an old '45. Gene Kelly, Leslie Caron, *An American in Paris*.

'Our Love is Here to Stay?' Spike said.

'You know it?'

'I've listened to Radio Gibraltar on more than one occasion, yes.'

She laid the record on the turntable.

'You're not going to sing again, are you?' The soft crackle immediately transported Spike back to his childhood, his mother humming along to Puccini as she cooked. Then Gene Kelly's rich voice started to croon the first of Gershwin's lyric, promising a love that would endure – outlast even the Rock of Gibraltar.

When Spike looked back, Amy was holding a photo frame that she'd picked up from the sideboard. Her wedding day, he realised as he approached – veil back, luminous face tilted upwards to kiss her husband. Grainger was a brute of a man, Spike saw now, broad-shouldered with a shaven scalp, folds of fat corrugating the back of his neck. The beast appeared to have been tamed, however: he looked almost vulnerable as he cradled his wife's head, wedding band squeezed around his thick ring finger.

Amy's large eyes were wet with tears. Spike smelled the clean sweet scent of her hair as he reached out and took her hand. 'May I?'

It wasn't clear who made the first move, but suddenly her mouth was pressed to his. He felt her drawing him close, her hips slotting into his as he bent his knees. Gene Kelly had moved on to a less familiar song by the time she led him to the sofa, drawing him down onto the heavy worn cushions.

Later, the only sound was the knocking of the record stylus and her gentle breathing. Spike banished thoughts of Zahra from his mind, then closed his eyes.

Chapter Twenty-nine

The ceiling above was a flaking magnolia pink. The smell was of rosewater. Spike twisted his head to the right. Beside him on the bed lay his client, Mrs Amy Grainger.

Spike rolled his eyes back to the ceiling, images flipping through his mind like a deck of cards – sitting on a beach in Cádiz with Jessica, the sound of his front door closing, dancing with Amy as she wept, her small hand in his as she'd led him from the sofa to the bedroom . . . He shifted position, head protesting at the movement. Amy was hugging a pillow to her chest like a child with a soft toy, her thin shoulders pale and naked beneath the duvet. Christ. He had to get out of here.

Her face in repose was even more beautiful, he noticed as he edged out of bed: full lips, black hair shading her white brow. He rolled to his feet. She didn't stir.

He reached for his T-shirt, smelling her scent in the cotton as he pulled it over his head. An aggressive buzzing came from the floor. He searched desperately for his trousers, grabbed his phone from his pocket and switched it off with a rigid thumb just as a new text message icon winked on the screen. He turned back to the bed. Still sleeping.

The light between the bedroom curtains was weak, dawn barely broken. Spike crept towards the door, one red espadrille in each hand, passing a collage of photos on the wall. All showed the happy couple, on a beach, at a restaurant, arm-in-arm with a volcanic green mountain behind – Thailand, maybe. In one corner lay a pair of slippers – monkeys forming the shoe, a snout at the toe and a tail at the heel. About Amy's size, Spike thought, wondering if Simon Grainger had given them to her as a present.

Spike's hand extended for the doorknob. There was a tremor to his fingers: must have had more than just wine last night. He groaned inwardly as he remembered the whisky he'd drunk with Jessica, the extra glass downed for Dutch courage before he'd left.

Amy's smooth back was still turned to him as he risked a final glance before easing into the sitting room. As he tiptoed round in relief, he found the little boy standing just a metre away, bare-foot, his dark brown hair mussed with sleep, washed-out blue and red pyjamas too short for his legs. He lifted his hands, a picture-board book clamped between them. 'Book?' he said. Spike hadn't even known a child his age could speak.

'Book?' he repeated, quietly insistent.

Spike put a finger to his lips.

'Book?'

'OK, OK,' Spike hissed, moving to the nearest sofa. Beneath the coffee table lay a condom wrapper greedily ripped in two; Spike kicked it beneath the valance as the boy tossed the book onto the sofa, raising his arms like a tiny, tyrannical gymnast. 'Up?'

Spike's eye was caught by a bottle of medicine on the side-board: 'Calpol', the label said. He unscrewed the top and took a gulp. When he opened his eyes again, the boy still stood at his feet. '*Up*?'

Gingerly, Spike picked the child up, feeling his brittle ribs beneath the warm cotton of his pyjamas. His little feet dangled between Spike's legs as he placed him on his lap, ankles twitching in anticipation.

'Row, Row, Row,' Spike read aloud as he turned the page. On one side of the double spread were the words of the nursery rhyme, on the other a picture of a teddy bear in a wooden skiff. 'Row, row, row your boat,' Spike continued, but the little boy twisted his head towards him, narrowing his dark eyes in fury. Spike took a breath, then reluctantly launched into quiet song. 'Gently down the stream . . .' he chimed, and the little face turned back to the book, a faint set of victory about the jaw.

'Merrily, merrily, merrily, *merrily* . . .'

The boy turned the next page himself. '. . . life is but a dream.' The top of the boy's head brushed against the underside of Spike's chin, his hair as silken and sweet as his mother's. Spike had a clear flashback: sitting on his father's knee, the sandpaper of his stubble as he bent down to kiss him, a little painful yet strangely comforting.

He assumed this was the end of the book, but no, more pages had further variations on the rowing theme. 'Gently to the shore . . . if you see a lion, don't forget to roar.'

The boy gave a small growl.

'Row, row, row your boat, out into the bay . . .' Now Teddy sat in a skiff with a skull and crossbones on the mast. He wore a cutlass at his side and a dashing eyepatch. 'If you see a pirate ship . . .'

'Row the other way?'

Spike's head thudded as he span round. Standing in the doorway was Amy Grainger. 'Mama!' Charlie shouted and rolled off Spike.

'A singer *and* a dancer,' Amy said. 'Who knew?' She wore a man's long white T-shirt. Spike forced a smile.

'Papi?' Charlie said, clinging to his mother's legs. Spike felt his stomach churn as his eyes flitted to the front door.

'Where Papi, Mama?'

Spike moved his gaze from mother to son. Both were as pale as paper. 'I'm sorry,' he mouthed. 'I have to go.'

Chapter Thirty

Spike kept to the lee of the Rock, glad of its shadow, shame curdling in his gut. A grocery store was opening for business, the Moroccan owner slopping down the pavement outside. Spike had intended to buy milk but the fridge was out of order. He took out a warm bottle of mineral water instead. 'Twenty-five pence,' the Moroccan said with a smile. The knowledge that the same drink would have cost a pound on Main Street did little to lift his mood.

Work, Spike thought as he drained the bottle and threw it in the bin – that was where salvation lay. In twenty-four hours he'd be on his way to court. He rubbed the back of his head, trying to ascertain if the water had eased his hangover. Not enough to suggest he'd feel much better tomorrow.

The neighbour's budgie was taunting a house sparrow as Spike unlocked the front door to find his father sitting at the kitchen table.

'Been somewhere nice?' Rufus said, spoon submerged in a bowl of cornflakes.

Spike raised the carton of milk from the table. Long-life, he realised as he gulped it down. If Spike didn't buy fresh food, it didn't get bought. 'I'm going upstairs.'

'I shan't disturb you then,' Rufus said. 'By the way,' he added as Spike passed. 'I solved your clue.'

'What clue?'

'The crossword clue you left on the table.'

Spike turned painfully from the bead curtain.

'F__S S__CT__ M_N__S,' Rufus read out. 'FLOS SANCTUS MONTIS. Nothing else fits.'

Spike peered down and saw the sheet of paper on which he'd written the letters from the ship's bell.

'It's Latin for "Holy Flower of the Mountain".'

'I know what it means, Dad,' Spike said, hearing the tetchy adolescent in his voice.

'It's the name of a ship,' Rufus went on, pushing back his mane of silver hair, a schoolmaster's vanity swelling his tone. He wore the same mauve silk dressing gown given to him twenty years ago by Spike's mother. What had once seemed embarrassingly patrician now just looked shabby. 'She was an old Spanish galleon, if I recall correctly. Named at a time when the Spanish still held Gibraltar. The Brits claim she sank in the Straits. Disputed by Spain, naturally.'

'When was this?'

'1720s, 30s maybe. It's all in the Garrison Library.' He tightened his dressing gown, then returned to his cornflakes.

Spike moved behind him and kissed the crown of his head.

'What's that?' Rufus said, looking up. 'Oh, my pleasure. It's all I'm good for these days.'

Chapter Thirty-one

As soon as Spike closed his bedroom door, he emailed his cousin, Sandra Zammit, at the Garrison Library to ask what she knew about the *Flos Sanctus Montis*. If the bell had really come from a famous ship, perhaps it could be worth something after all. It was a Sunday, he realised as he hit send, but at least she would get the message on Monday morning.

Composing himself, he took out his skeleton argument for the Neptune case. The print danced in tune with the throbbing of his head. So much for Calpol. He found three aspirin in his bathroom, gulped them down and took a shower.

Downstairs, Rufus was singing along to an aria from *Turandot*. Spike sat back down at his desk, almost refreshed. He stared at the drawer, then pulled it open and found the sheaf of his mother's letters inside. He knew it wouldn't improve his mood, but somehow he couldn't help it.

'*My dearest J – Yesterday we caught the ferry to the Île de Ré. I could see R watching me, pointing out the beaches, the strange paddy fields where they harvest the sea salt. He is so desperate to see me smile, to remind me of the fun we had here on our honeymoon. But I just can't do it. Because my mind is lost to you, my love. You are always in my thoughts . . .*'

'Focus, for fuck's sake,' Spike cursed, putting the letter away. Slowly, his mind began to flesh out the bullet points into sentences and paragraphs. It was important for a barrister not to write everything down, Peter always said, or he could sound stilted.

Know what you're going to say, not how you're going to say it. Half an hour passed, and Spike felt himself turning back into a lawyer who'd been out the night before, rather than a drunkard masquerading as a lawyer. Outside, he heard the Church of the Sacred Heart chime eleven. He eyed the desk drawer again, then reached for his mobile and lay back on his bed.

His phone was still off from when he'd silenced it in Amy's flat. Two new texts, the first with an Italian title – '*Ecco l'uomo*', *Here is the man* – and a photograph attached. Sender: Enrico Sanguinetti. Spike smiled as he clicked on the file. The picture took a while to download; when it finally did, it appeared to have been shot surreptitiously from waist-height, as the lens was angled upwards. It showed a man walking along what looked like a hotel corridor. Only his upper half was captured, but the quality was good, well worth the 100 euros Spike had promised. The man looked about fifty, pale and craggy, with a pointed chin and intelligent brown eyes, one of which had a slight droop. His nose was strong, his hair dark, maybe a tad too dark for his age, cut short around the ears. He wore a thin leather jacket, casual against the opulent red carpet and expensive wallpaper of the hotel. His left arm was hooked proprietorially around a woman's elbow, someone a little taller than him, judging by the upwards slant. Spike scrolled to the right. A slender forearm was visible, bronzed, fine-boned, the wrist adorned by three chunky silver bangles, linked together like a Russian wedding ring. Spike knew the arm belonged to Zahra before he'd even zoomed in. And there it was, the thin white scar on the back of her hand, a mark he'd once put to his lips as she'd told him of its unexciting provenance. He zoomed back out: Žigon's lazy eye was clear and cold, peering downwards, perhaps to where the camera lay. She's mine, it seemed say, and there's nothing you can do about it.

'Well, that's it, then,' Spike muttered.

He closed the attachment, then remembered the second text. Another photograph. Would this one show her face? He clicked on the icon, finding himself humming 'Row, row, row your boat' as the picture downloaded. Then he saw its contents and dropped his phone.

Enrico's yellow front teeth protruded rodent-like above his lower lip. His red doorman's hat lay on the floor by his left ear, newspaper spread out beneath. The collar of his shirt was undone, and above his thick chest hair, Spike made out a wide dark gash, at least five inches long, running from one side of his neck to the other, the cartilaginous white of a windpipe gleaming through the bloody mush. Spike's eyes were drawn to the left, protesting at the terrible thing curled up inside Enrico's hat. A long grey root, pale speckles on the bloodstained skin. Now Spike realised why Enrico's front teeth had been so visible. His tongue had been cut out.

Spike's eyes began to ache. He sensed the blood draining from his cheeks, rushing to his organs. He could tell he was going to be sick, but couldn't seem to move. A third text arrived; he heard the double-beep, then saw his fingertip jab down clumsily at the key.

'*You were warned. We are watching you and your family. Do not tell anybody. If you alert the police we will know. Someone will come for your phone.*'

Spike slumped off the bed and crawled to the bathroom. Rolling onto his side, he laid his cheek to the cold tiles, concentrating on his breathing, waiting for the nausea to ease. Then a new panic started to fill his belly as he realised that he'd been lying there for five minutes and no noise had come from downstairs. He lurched out onto the landing and sprinted down the stairs, damp soles skidding through the bead curtain and into the kitchen. 'Dad!'

A note lay on the kitchen table: 'Gone to get the papers.' Chest still heaving, Spike steadied himself on the chair back. Slowly, numbly, he started to realise how far he had strayed out of his depth. His mind ranged through the people he might go to for help: Galliano, Zahra, Jessica . . . He almost laughed. *If you alert the police we will know.* The last warning he'd ignored. And now Peter lay comatose in hospital. Enrico was dead, tortured then killed. Who would be next? Zahra? Rufus? Maybe Spike could leave Gibraltar – cross the border to Spain and catch a train north. Impossible. They wanted the phone. It was the photograph of Žigon they were after. If Spike ran away, then someone else could get hurt.

Outside, the church bell began to toll. In less than twenty-two hours, Spike realised, he would be standing before a judge in court.

*

I sit down reluctantly on the red section of the Union-Jack-painted kerb, reading a tourist map, browsing the local ads – 'Rock Tours by Taxi: Visit Gib with the People who Know'; 'Dolphin World – THE best dolphin safaris, come and find us at Ocean Village'; 'World War II Tunnels – See where thousands of people lived and worked deep inside the Rock – Walk through History!' There is movement inside the door of the tower block; I get to my feet to see a fat man shuffling down the internal stairs. He checks his pigeonhole, then switches on a handheld fan and minces out onto the street.

I sit back down. Interspersed with the parochial ads are notices for private banks, law firms, hedge funds. I wonder if the seaside facade the colony affects is a deliberate cover for financial impropriety. Not that there's much high finance happening in this part of town, I think, as I glance around the estate, which seems to have been built on top of a castle, no doubt a fine old Spanish fortress pulled down by the British.

More footsteps. This one looks different. Pretty, young, doe-eyed. Out of place. She pulls a handful of letters from her pigeonhole, and I creep closer: Flat 7B, the sign on the wooden box says. Bingo.

'Charlie?' I hear the woman call up the stairs. 'Hurry up.'

She exits to the forecourt. A few moments later, a small boy appears, face set with concentration as he runs unsteadily to catch her up.

The child complicates matters. But complicated does not mean impossible. I wait until they are out of sight, then start up the stairs towards the seventh floor.

Chapter Thirty-two

'It seems to me,' said Judge Bossano, 'that this morning's hearing can be considered in two parts. The first is relatively simple, and I shall pronounce on it now in the same way that the Receiver of Wreck would have done.'

Bossano peered down from his bench. On this of all days, Spike found himself before the most belligerent judge in Gibraltar. He found his eyes inching down from Bossano's face to the stiff winged collar around his neck, prompting a sickening image of the jagged cartilage of Enrico Sanguinetti's throat to flicker through his mind. The picture must have been a fake, Spike told himself again. Fabricated to stop him digging deeper. That was all that had happened. Nothing to worry about.

Bossano was glaring at him now, wig skewed, massive ego demanding the court's full attention. 'The Claimant posits that the *Gloucester* was engaged on military business when she sank,' he resumed. 'The Ministry of Defence therefore has clear title to the cargo of lead. I believe that the MoD has already reached an agreement with Neptune Marine to that effect, which is not under dispute from the Crown?' Bossano glanced at Drew Stanford-Trench, the barrister representing the interests of Customs and Excise.

'No dispute, my Lord,' Stanford-Trench said, eyeing Spike as he knocked a document wallet off his desk.

'Where the real complexity lies,' the judge went on, 'is with the discovery of the unlisted cargo of silver bullion. Mr Sanguinetti – perhaps you might elucidate this for the Court?'

Bossano topped up his glass with sparkling mineral water, then sat back in his red leather chair, broad forearms spread across the bench. Like Spike, he'd come up through the Mags, and appeared to be relishing the more generous appointment of the Supreme Court.

'Absolutely, my Lord,' Spike replied, rising carefully to his feet. In the row behind, he sensed the keen gaze of Clohessy and Jardine trained upon him. 'My client, Neptune Marine, is one of the foremost maritime salvage companies in the world. Having identified a potential wreck site in Gibraltarian territorial waters, they fulfilled the Duties of Finder as set out in the Merchant Shipping Act of 1894, then began their deepwater investigations, only to come unexpectedly upon a safe on the seabed containing more than a thousand bars of unmarked silver. Rather than act unscrupulously, Neptune immediately informed the Receiver of Wreck, who asked the Court to pronounce on the matter of ownership. As Neptune had instructed my colleague, Peter Galliano, who was sadly taken ill last month' – Bossano gave a sober nod; he and Peter were friends, it was a shameless name-drop, but one Peter would have appreciated – 'it has fallen to me to step in on his behalf. Whilst awaiting the hearing date, my client placed advertisements in both *Lloyd's List* and Ukrainian *Pravda* asking for any heirs to the silver to declare themselves. As his Lordship can now see from Document B, no credible heir has emerged.' The judge moistened his lower lip in concentration as he examined the sheet, and Spike found himself staring at the pink tip of his tongue . . .

'Mr Sanguinetti?'

He looked back at his papers, struggling to locate his train of thought. His horsehair wig itched at his temples and his black gown felt unbearably hot and heavy. Behind, he heard someone hiss something in a Canadian accent. He needed to pull himself together . . . 'The fact is, my Lord,' Spike said, abandoning his notes, 'that the silver bars in question were being illegally smuggled. I can therefore surmise what my learned friend here will try and argue.' Stanford-Trench's handsome face took on an amused expression – he was a far more dangerous opponent now that he'd fallen in love and given up the drink.

'He will tell you,' Spike continued, 'that under section 241 (1) of the MSA, Customs and Excise enjoys the same right to confiscate the silver today as had they intercepted the ship back in 1853.'

'Let's leave Mr Stanford-Trench to make his own submissions, shall we?'

'Very well. Can I therefore ask the Court to turn to Document D?'

Bossano flicked through the bundle Spike had submitted.

'On page 32, you will see that the principle of "treasure trove" has been an integral part of English common law since the time of Edward the Confessor. If treasure has been deliberately concealed with intent to retrieve, then it belongs automatically to the Crown. However, if treasure is lost or abandoned, then whoever finds it enjoys the right to keep it.'

Bossano nodded as he scanned the case law.

'We would argue that in this case, as the silver has been lost, rather than deliberately concealed, the principle of "treasure trove" applies.'

The judge began scribbling down notes. 'And this is not just any finder we are talking about,' Spike went on. 'Neptune Marine has dedicated over a year of resources to this project. To say nothing of enormous financial expenditure. Each day spent in possession of the wreck site costs them over £35,000. Not only have they been moored now in the Straits for more than three weeks, but they have faced continual harassment from the Guardia Civil, who claim incorrectly that their ship is trespassing in Spanish waters. Meanwhile, the firm's value on the Toronto Stock Exchange has been falling. Such risks as those undertaken by my client in today's economic climate should be rewarded. It speaks volumes that the MoD in Gibraltar is not pressing a claim on the silver. After all, the costs and hazards are borne by Neptune Marine alone.' Spike looked back to Drew Stanford-Trench, but opposing counsel had his head down now, diligently preparing his response.

'In conclusion,' Spike said, 'my client's claim on the silver has support both in law, under the "treasure trove" principle, and in equity, given the investment they have made. Hard work,' he added, addressing the courtroom, 'deserves its reward.' He sat back down, feeling his head start to swim. 'Mr Sanguinetti?' he heard as if through water.

He hauled himself back up. 'My Lord?'

'What thought has been given to storage?'

'Storage?'

'Given the high value of the lead, and particularly the silver, the Court needs to be assured that a secure storage facility has been identified. You can't just lock this sort of thing up in a garage.'

Spike felt a tug at his gown. 'One moment, my Lord,' he said, turning to find Jardine's outstretched arm clutching a scrap of paper. Some kind of diagram and a scrawled note. The lines began to blur. 'I must beg the Court's indulgence while I confer with my client on this point.'

'Lunchtime draws ever closer, Mr Sanguinetti,' Bossano said. 'Let's hear from Mr Stanford-Trench.'

Drew Stanford-Trench stood up with a confident smile. 'My Lord, as we have just heard from opposing counsel, for which many thanks, under section 241 (1) of the Merchant Shipping Act . . .'

Clohessy and Jardine were huddled together as Spike shunted his chair round. 'We *talked* about this,' Clohessy whispered.

'It's a map of the Stay Behind Cave,' Jardine said. Spike caught a whiff of booze in the air; he hoped it was coming from Jardine. 'Tell me you've heard of it?'

Every Gibraltarian had. In the Second World War, the Allies had been so convinced Hitler would invade Gibraltar that they had created a secret fortified bunker in the Rock, fitted out for ten men to 'stay behind' and send back crucial intelligence if Gib was captured. A team had even been selected to man it, trained in endurance techniques by a survivor of Scott's Antarctic expedition. But Hitler had attacked Russia instead, and the bunker had been consigned to history.

'The MoD is letting Neptune store the lead there,' Jardine said. 'There's bags of room for the silver.'

'We talked about this,' Clohessy repeated.

'Maybe to Peter, not to me,' Spike snapped, causing Stanford-Trench to break off from his monologue. Just let this be over, Spike willed, more grateful then ever for the courts' Summer Hours. 'How many days do you need?' he asked.

'Two to bring up the cargo,' Clohessy said, 'so long as the weather holds. Another day to pack it up. Then we fly it all to Vancouver by private jet. Four in total, at the most.'

'What's your insurer's position?'

'Zurich's over the fucking moon,' Clohessy hissed. 'The cave's the most secure place on the Rock.'

Spike moved his chair round to find Stanford-Trench elegantly bringing his submission to a close.

'Mr Sanguinetti?' Bossano said, emptying his bottle of water.

Spike explained to the judge about the bunker, then watched him bang his papers on the bench like a gavel. 'Thank you. The Court will now relay its verdict.'

Chapter Thirty-three

Spike stepped out of the portico into the punishing midday heat. He thought that he'd tarried long enough in the changing rooms for everyone connected to the case to have left. Not so: Hugh Jardine was standing in the shade of one of the giant date palms laid out when the Law Courts had been built in the 1830s. He turned away from the court notice board, narrow grey eyes protected by an elderly pair of Wayfarers. In his cream suit he had the louche look of a James Bond actor put out to pasture, then called unexpectedly back into service.

'I hadn't realised they tried the *Mary Celeste* case here,' he called out. 'You'd have solved that one, wouldn't you, Somerset?' He smiled and lit a cigarette.

There was something of Rufus's leanness about Jardine, Spike thought, though none of his intelligence. Spike managed a perfunctory nod, then continued down the gravel path towards the street.

Flitting between the garden's wrought-iron gates was Mort Clohessy, mobile phone clamped to ear, jawbone bulging, two fingers wrenching loose his Hermès tie. He looked as uncomfortable in a suit as Jardine had looked at home – a Tour de France winner forced into black tie for an awards dinner.

'I don't gave two shits what it costs,' he barked, 'I want it chartered and parked on the runway for as long it takes. I'll call a board meeting if I have to.' He saw Spike and beckoned him over. 'Too damned right,' he concluded to the unfortunate at the end of the line.

Slipping the phone into his suit pocket, Clohessy pulled off his tinted glasses. Then he held out his arms and croaked with as much warmth as he could muster, 'You just saved my company, bud.'

Clohessy's sinewy arms felt like leather straps around Spike's back. He drew out of the embrace earlier than might have been considered friendly.

'Mr Sanguinetti doesn't look too happy about it,' Jardine called over, tapping his ash into a bed of orchids.

'Shut the fuck up, Hugh,' Clohessy said, teeth bared in a smile. 'You kicked ass, Sanguinetti.'

'Just doing my job,' Spike replied. Someone jostled him from behind and he leapt to one side in alarm. A family of Sephardis late for Synagogue, the father with an 'Arsenal Football Club' logo embroidered onto his skull cap.

'I'm taking the crew out later in Ocean Village,' Clohessy went on. 'You'll join us.'

'I'm afraid I'm busy. But thank you.'

'Six p.m. at Ipanema's.'

'Sorry,' Spike said, but Clohessy wasn't listening now, taking out his phone to answer another call.

Spike turned and set off down Main Street, vaguely aware of Jardine still watching him from the gatepost. Spike wanted to knock the slim-eyed smile off his face. A moment later he heard his name. He ignored it but the call came again, 'Spike?'

Drew Stanford-Trench held a beaded Coke can, bought from the café by the Law Courts. He caught Spike up. 'Jesus, Spike! Didn't you hear me?' A look of concern clouded his clever freckled face. No lawyer with such a fair complexion should ever have moved to the Rock, Spike thought, however calamitous their degree result.

'What's with the doomed expression?' Stanford-Trench said.

'Not feeling so good today, Drew.'

'Beaten by a man with a weapons-grade hangover,' Stanford-Trench chuckled, shaking his head. 'Fancy some lunch? Settle the stomach?'

'I think I'll just go home.'

'I can walk with you as far as the Cathedral?'

Spike glanced down the street. The Sephardis were gone, replaced by day-trippers heading for the cable car, wafting programme sheets against their faces in a vain attempt to cool down.

'Actually, I'd rather you didn't.'

Stanford-Trench took a step back. 'OK.'

'It's just not a good time.'

He nodded, then laid a hand on Spike's arm. 'You know you can always talk to me, Spike. Whatever's wrong, I guarantee I've seen worse.'

Spike nodded back. No mention had been made of the shoddy trick Spike had pulled in court, pre-empting his opponent's argument. He squeezed Stanford-Trench's shoulder gratefully, then turned off Main Street into the less crowded alleys above.

His phone was ringing. He swallowed drily, expecting to see Enrico Sanguinetti's number on the screen. Instead, Jessica Navarro's face smiled back. He knew that if he didn't answer she'd hunt him down, turn up unannounced at his house. Gibraltar suddenly felt oppressively small.

'Hey,' Jessica said. The silence made it clear that the onus was on Spike to speak. 'You OK?' he offered eventually.

'We need to talk.'

'Fire away.'

'Face to face.'

Spike looked to his left. Something had moved at the periphery of his vision – just a man on a scooter with two fishing rods on his shoulders. 'I'm sorry, Jess. I can't at the moment.' He felt her hurt reverberate down the line. 'Listen. You're . . .'

'What?' she said, anger ignited.

He felt his voice start to shake. He raised his head, seeing an arm cut out against the blue sky as a hand reached from a top-floor window to adjust a satellite dish on the roof. 'You're the best person I know, Jess. But right now, I really need you to leave me alone.'

Phone clenched in his fist, Spike turned onto Cannon Lane, waiting for the next message from Enrico Sanguinetti, or for a stranger to appear at the next corner. High above the Old Town, the Rock stared down impassively.

Chapter Thirty-four

Rufus stood hunched in the kitchen, still in his mauve dressing gown, peering into the fridge as though lunch might mysteriously appear. On the table behind him lay the *Chronicle*'s cryptic crossword. An editorial connecting Alfred Benady's death to Peter Galliano's hit-and-run dominated the opposite page: 'Call for Speed Cameras on Gib's Steep Backstreets', the headline screamed.

'Don't you ever get dressed?' Spike said, more sharply than he'd intended.

Rufus turned from the fridge, appraising the tension in his son's face. His dressing gown gaped, revealing a frail pigeon chest – combined with his height, a classic symptom of Marfan syndrome, the doctors had said, amazed that no one had picked it up before. Under his armpit ran the lurid scar where a tube had been inserted last year to drain his lungs. 'Woman trouble?' he asked as he closed the fridge with his long, spindly fingers.

'I'm sorry?'

'You've been in a foul mood for days,' he went on. '*Cherchez la femme . . .*' He sat down, mulling a clue. 'Don't know how to keep 'em happy, I s'pose.'

'And you'd know all about that,' Spike murmured.

Rufus peered up over his half-moons, and Spike took in the hearing aid built into their frame, feeling irritation tighten his jaw.

'I beg your pardon?' Rufus said.

As Spike gazed at his father's blithe face, he realised that ever since Rufus's diagnosis he'd been reluctant to speak plainly, afraid of upsetting him. Of making things worse. 'Who's "J"?'

'Jay who?'

'The letter "J". Comes after I, as a rule. He was mentioned a great deal in those airmail letters you dug out of the attic. From Mum. Someone she cared for quite a lot, it would seem.'

There was a pause, then Rufus said quietly, 'Whereof one cannot speak, thereof one must be silent.'

'Is that a clue or a reply?'

Rufus set his pen down on the table.

'You might kid yourself that you were a good husband, Dad. But not only did your wife kill herself, it seems that she was having an affair right under your nose.'

Suddenly Rufus slammed down his palms, a gesture Spike knew had wrought terror in the hearts of thousands of adolescent pupils. Dragging himself to his feet, he lurched towards his son, right arm raised. He had never hit Spike during his childhood, but then again, he'd never had the chance – Spike had always been halfway up the stairs before the shouting had even started. Lifting a hand into the air, Spike caught Rufus's thin wrist, feeling his anger dissipate as he watched the pain flash across his father's face. Shame and weariness filling the void, Spike sat down on one of the old wooden chairs and pulled one out for Rufus. 'Come on, Dad. Let's have something to eat.'

Chapter Thirty-five

'*Whereof one cannot speak, thereof one must be silent*' . . . Typical of Rufus to hide behind somebody else's line. Spike sat down on his bed and took out his phone. Clicking open the text message, he forced himself to reread it: *You were warned. We are watching you and your family. Do not tell anybody. If you alert the police we will know. Someone will come for your phone.*

So Zahra had been right. Why had he doubted her? She'd been nothing but straight with him for as long as he'd known her. And what if by ignoring her warning he had put her in greater danger? From now on, he would just do as he was told. Hand over the phone and hope for the best. He couldn't allow anyone else to be put at risk.

Feeling the dizziness start to return, he opened his email, trying to ignore the reams of work-related messages that were starting to clog up his inbox. Tomorrow he was meant to be meeting Peter Galliano's sister to discuss his 'future'. An ill-chosen word: the discussion would focus on whether or not the doctors should let him die. Finding little comfort in the fact that there were still some people worse off than himself, he scrolled through the rest of his messages, stopping when he found one from Sandra Zammit at the Garrison Library entitled 'Flos Sanctus Montis'.

'Hi Cuz,' it began. Spike smiled despite himself at Sandra's writing style – more akin to that of a teenager than a 62-year-old. Perhaps a reaction to spending too long around antique books. 'U R 2nd person wanting info on this. All we have is copy of original manifest. Booked out at mo but I will let u no when its back. Sandra.'

Spike immediately called the Garrison Library, picturing the Bakelite telephone pealing away unattended in the back room. The library had been founded in 1793 to provide reading material for officers during lengthy Spanish sieges, and sometimes it felt like it had barely advanced since then.

'Garrison Library, 418?' came a hesitant voice.

'Sandra. It's Spike.'

'Sorry?'

'Spike Sanguinetti. Your cousin.'

'How lovely. You got my message then?'

'I did. And I was wondering – who booked out the manifest?'

'I'm afraid I can't say. Data protection.'

'Oh come on, Sandra . . .'

Spike heard gentle breathing, then the receiver laid down and the hum of a radio behind. 'Just because it's you, Spike,' Sandra resumed. 'It's out to a . . . Peter Galliano.'

Spike felt a sudden rush of confusion. 'Really? When?'

'Three weeks ago.'

Around the time of the hit-and-run, Spike thought.

'I remember him coming in. Nice man – big smile. Told me it was do with a case he was working on. Isn't he connected to you in some way?'

'We work together. Do you have another copy of the manifest?'

'Just the one. I was amazed we had it at all. Something to do with a controversy over whether she sank or not.'

'Is there anything else about the ship?'

'How funny! That's exactly what your colleague asked. The answer was no.'

'Do you know where I can find more information?'

'You could check the law library.'

'I already have.'

'Or the "internet" maybe?' She said the word as if he might not have heard of it and she'd only recently added it to her vocabulary.

'There's nothing there.'

'Then you'll just have to find someone who knows about boats. Listen, Spike, you should pop by some time. Our dragon tree is coming into bloom.'

Spike fought an urge to join his cousin in the library's shady back garden and get quietly smashed on G&Ts.

'Or ask your Pa. Expect he could use the company.'

'I'll mention it. Thanks, Sandra.'

His finger moved towards Amy Grainger's number, then he dismissed the idea, remembering Charlie's earnest face peering up at him. Instead he went downstairs, catching sight of his silent father's back. Still seated at the table – brooding no doubt.

Once at Chambers, he searched through Galliano's filing cabinet but found no sign of the ship's manifest, just the stuffed Spanish wildcat gazing down from the windowsill, trapped, frozen. Talk to someone who knows about boats, Sandra Zammit had said. Well, Spike thought, checking the time, and feeling grateful for the distraction. That he could do.

Chapter Thirty-six

Though Ocean Village lay just on the other side of the peninsula to the Moorish Castle Estate, it might have been on a different continent. The development had been built to service the wealthy yachting crowd in the hope that they might berth their boats there, or use it as a stopover when sailing in and out of the Med. A sparkling new apartment plaza – in a building shaped like the Rock itself – rose at the shoreline, along with a business centre and a Gala casino where you could drink for free and lose whatever you'd earned next door. The most interesting element was the mode of land reclamation, a series of long wooden pontoons stretching into the bay, each leading to an 'internationally themed' restaurant or nightclub.

A tanned couple in white shorts and silver Oakley shades were carrying a box of provisions from the local yacht-supply shop. Spike stopped to let them climb down to their berth, then continued along the slatted walkway. Fat bamboo poles draped with fisherman's rope served as banisters. The water below was lit up, revealing the snub-nosed silhouettes of grey mullet cruising the blue-green murk. 'Leisure Island', as the authorities dubbed it, was staggeringly tasteless in Spike's view, but on more than one occasion, after the pubs of the Old Town had closed, he had been grateful for its late-night bars. O'Reilly's offered cod Irish gaiety, Le Petit Café, misspelt 'coque au vin', The Cuban, a half-decent mojito. As far as Spike knew, Celebrities Wine Bar ('Buy 5 Coronas Get 1 Free') was yet to attract any of its namesakes. He wondered which of the establishments Simon Grainger had worked at.

Clohessy had chosen what was probably the pick of the bunch – Ipanema's, a Brazilian-themed restaurant selling British beer on tap. As Spike approached, he noticed the *Trident*'s sleek inflatable tender moored in one of the berths. Perched on a bamboo bench above, a lone man sat staring out at the Straits. At first Spike thought it was the Scottish driver of the RIB, Dougie, but finding he was mistaken, he walked past him into the restaurant.

The best place to sit was outside, in an open-sided cabaña rising from the decking. Sure enough, Clohessy and the Neptune crew were there, clustered around the semicircular bar as a table was laid up behind them. Being welcomed in by this large group of capable, unflappable men felt strangely reassuring.

'You made it,' Clohessy called out in his nasal accent, raising an iced hi-ball tumbler. He was back in the clothes that made him comfortable, thin manmade fibres that could probably withstand any extreme of temperature. His colleagues were also in mufti, the occasional Hawaiian shirt revealing 'characters' within the group who had hitherto seemed dour. 'Johnnie, fix this man a drink,' Clohessy said, and the younger of the Scottish brothers, ever eager to please, turned a glass a violent purple with one of the jugs on the bar.

'Walk with me,' Clohessy said, passing Spike his drink. It was an amiable order rather than a request. He pressed a hand to Spike's back as they moved to the edge of the decking. 'Mike's still aboard,' he said, pointing with his glass in the direction of the *Trident*. 'We begin the salvage at 6 a.m.'

Spike plucked the fluorescent cocktail umbrella from his glass and took a sip. The drink was so sweet it was hard to know what wasn't in it.

'I meant what I said before,' Clohessy resumed. 'I've earned a heck of a lot of money in my time, and I've always prided myself on making things. Useful things that last. But I've put my soul into Neptune. There's beauty hidden on the seabed, and we need it up here, enriching our culture, safeguarding our history.

Injecting much-needed capital into the economy.' Into your bank account, Spike thought. 'We've had ten good years at Neptune, but technology keeps moving on. We had to float the business last year. Raise more investment. My ass is on the line with the shareholders. I owe a ton of alimony to my ex-wife. If you hadn't pulled this off . . .' He turned to survey his employees; Jardine was there now, raising a glass. 'Well, I could have been pushed out of the company I founded. It's happened before.' He looked back at Spike. 'You're one hell of an advocate, Sanguinetti.'

'How much do you know about ships' bells?'

A small frown wrinkled Clohessy's tanned brow. 'What do you mean?'

'A friend has come across one and I'm keen to find out more.'

'Jamie?' Clohessy called to the bar.

His timid public schoolboy emerged from the throng. 'Mr Sanguinetti has some technical questions. Answer them, would you?' He patted Spike again on the back. 'I'm gonna chase up the food. Sometimes you Brits don't put enough spice on the chicken wings.'

Jamie lingered at Spike's shoulder. His cocktail umbrella was still in place; he took a sip, canopy pressing against his weak goatee.

'I was asking Mort about ships' bells.'

Jamie wiped his mouth, immediately surer of his ground. 'They're like gold dust for us, Mr Sanguinetti. Provide the best identifier of a shipwreck.'

'I see,' Spike said, though he didn't.

'A bell is an essential form of communication on a ship – you ring the bell every half-hour, and the watch of a sailor lasts eight bells. You've heard the phrase, Knock seven bells out of someone? Well, eight bells means the end of a shift, so seven bells is almost – but not quite – finished.' Jamie cast an uneasy look at Spike, perhaps realising he was straying off the point. 'In the old days, when a ship got into trouble, she would throw her cannons and ballast overboard, or cut her anchors. But the bell stayed put.' He took in Spike's vacant look and opted for a more binary explanation. 'Basically, Mr Sanguinetti, if a ship goes down, the bell goes with her. And the best bit? Not only do bells have the date they were cast engraved on them, they usually show the name of the vessel as well.'

'Have you heard of a ship called . . .'

Spike felt a prod in the back and turned to see Jardine standing behind him in a pressed pink shirt and chinos. The strength of the jab had suggested someone younger. 'In case you were wondering, there's not a drop of alcohol in that,' he said, pointing at Spike's glass. 'Mort's Law. He's a Presbyterian, you know.' Jamie took the opportunity to scurry back to the safety of the crowd as Jardine lit another of his ubiquitous cigarettes. Benson and Hedges, Spike noticed, remembering someone else who had smoked that brand. 'How well did you know my mother?' he asked, then immediately regretted it.

Jardine exhaled aromatically, then leaned in. 'Questions like that need the right kind of lubricant.' He smiled indulgently. 'Why don't I pop down to the boatie supply shop? Then we can have a proper chinwag.'

Spike watched him walk stiffly away down the wooden pier, noting his breadth of shoulder, trying to imagine what a woman might have seen in him twenty years ago.

'Food's up,' Clohessy called out.

An enormous tray of dangerous-looking chicken wings had been placed in the middle of the round table. Spike looked for Jamie, but it was Dougie who appeared at his elbow. 'Seat of honour, pal,' he said in his Scottish brogue, pulling out a chair.

Clohessy reappeared. As soon as he sat down, everyone followed. Licking his thin lips, Clohessy reached over and grabbed a fistful of wings. Spike wondered idly if he'd be throwing them up later.

'Hear you caned it in court today,' Dougie said, words fighting their way through his thick Glaswegian accent.

'We had a fair case,' Spike replied, glancing across the table to see Anders the Swede drawing a chicken wing through his white teeth, mouth smeared with sauce.

Clohessy began sketching something on the back of a napkin; he passed it to Stevo, the South African engineer, who nodded, then added something to the diagram.

'Mort?' Spike said.

Clohessy turned. There were eight neat little bones lying on his plate and a mild look of disgust on his face.

'I had another question.'

'Did Jamie not . . .'

'He did, but I wanted to ask you. Have you ever heard of a ship called the *Flos Sanctus Montis*?'

Clohessy's face reddened as the spice hit him. He raised his napkin to his island of brown hair. 'I don't think so.'

'The Holy Flower of the Mountain?'

Quiet fell around the table.

'What makes you ask?'

Spike watched Clohessy's small eyes assessing him from behind their spectacles. 'Nothing,' he said. 'Doesn't matter.'

The tray of chicken wings was almost empty. Spike had eaten nothing. Clohessy pushed his chair back, then whispered something to Stevo and left the restaurant. The waitress reappeared with a fresh jug of punch. Dougie gave her a lascivious wink, then slid what looked like a silver hipflask from the pocket of his shorts.

Spike heard a noise behind. He turned and saw Jardine standing on the pier, holding up a brown paper bag and knocking two plastic cups against it. Behind, outside the casino, the uplights had come on, red, white and blue bulbs illuminating a row of imported pine and olive trees.

'Excuse me,' Spike said to Dougie, but he was too busy eyeing up the waitress to listen.

Chapter Thirty-seven

Flashing Spike one of his laconic smiles, Hugh Jardine gestured at the bamboo bench behind the restaurant. Spike sat down beside him, and for a moment they both stared out in silence at the Bay of Gibraltar. The levanter was getting up again, charging the Straits with a swell. In the night sky, a small plane was banking round to land on the Rock's tiny single runway. Spike wondered if it was the private jet Clohessy had chartered.

Jardine reached for the paper bag. 'Time for a proper drop,' he said, rubbing his hands together like a housefly. 'You were asking me about your mother, weren't you?' he added as he expertly worked out the cork. 'Well, son, you don't need me to tell you that she was the most beautiful woman on the Rock . . .'

In the half-light, Spike heard rather than saw the sound of viscous liquid poured into glasses. 'Did you have an affair with her?'

The pouring stopped abruptly as Jardine spat out his bark of a laugh. 'Whatever gave you that idea?' Above the bay, the jet made its final approach. 'Well, she was certainly wasted on her husband,' Jardine continued, taking a sip of his drink as he fixed Spike with his laughing eyes.

Spike put the cup to his lips. The tepid liquor burned his throat as it made its way downwards, tasting much as he would have imagined neat methanol might. As he glanced down at the bottle beneath the bench, he caught sight of the label: Wood's Navy Rum. He started to pull himself to his feet, but Jardine reached out and grabbed his wrist.

'Not just yet, eh, son?'

Spike tried to wrench his arm away, then felt Jardine's middle finger digging into the top of his hand like a vice. 'Know how I came to be in Gibraltar?' he said.

Spike suppressed a cry of pain as the pressure increased. With his free hand, Jardine hoisted up the tail of his pink shirt. A purple, bubbling scar ran up the length of one flank. 'Darwin Hill, 1982, 2 Para,' he said. 'I couldn't fight any more so they sent me here.'

Spike tried to move his arm back, hoping to find the space to swing a punch, but now Jardine was pressing his thumb up into Spike's palm. An extraordinary pain ran through his hand like an electrical current, and he reared back in agony.

'No one in Westminster gives a toss about the locals on this godforsaken Rock,' Jardine said. 'It's about the Empire, and what's owed to us. Gib's a trinket and we'll keep it for as long as we want.' He released Spike's hand with a smile. 'Stop rooting about, that's my advice, young man. Stick to what you're best at – paperwork.' He picked up Spike's glass, sank the remainder then tossed the empty cup into the water. 'Thought this would be too strong a meat for you,' he said. 'Pretty boy. Just like your mother.'

Spike watched Jardine push his way back into the heaving restaurant. Then he turned and walked away down the pontoon.

*

I return armed with the proper tools – knife, credit card, something a bit special I've kept concealed in the secret compartment in the car. I have a quick listen at the door, then insert the blade beneath the latch, tilting it upwards as I slip the credit card inside. 'God Bless Our Home' pleads the tile by the bell-push. Indeed, I think to myself as I ease the door open.

On the self-assembled coffee table, a jigsaw lies half-completed, the Rock of Gibraltar sliced into cardboard chunks. My foot slides on a children's book. I kick it under the sofa and move into the bedroom.

Twisted, unmade sheets . . . I rifle through the chest of drawers and find the underwear: practical knickers, mainly. A couple of cheap lacy numbers. I try the drawer above and find what I'm looking for. The stocking stretches between my gloved hands with a taut denier gleam. Adequate – but I know I can do better.

As I move through the sitting room, I am unable to prevent myself from finishing the jigsaw, slotting piece after piece into place until the Rock glares back at me. The photographer has even caught a pall of low cloud on its peak. It's getting dark outside, I suddenly realise. More time has elapsed than I thought. I check the sideboard beneath the record player, then open all the storage units in the hall. My fingers hesitate over a shelf of unusual items. Artefacts, one might call them. Surprising in such an apartment.

A noise comes from outside, a key turning in the lock. 'You've been such a good boy,' I hear, 'let's not spoil it now . . .'

My hand darts into the cupboard and grabs a coil of rope. The yellow hemp feels slimy but the strength is excellent.

Childish chatter in the kitchenette, then her voice again, 'Charlie! You finished your puzzle and I didn't even see . . .'

I wait until she puts a record on the player – tasteless American crooning – then make my entrance.

Chapter Thirty-eight

Spike paced the strip-lit corridors of the hospital, mind shooting off in different directions, finding connections between events previously assumed disparate. The same nurse sat at the desk, this time occupied by form-filling rather than Facebook. 'He returns,' she said with an attempt at a dazzling smile.

'Did Peter have a briefcase with him?'

Her face fell. 'Sorry?'

'When he was admitted to hospital. Do you know if he had a briefcase?'

The nurse gave an anxious look. 'I'd have to check the property room . . .'

Spike could see her poised to object. 'He named me as next of kin. Along with his sister.'

She slowly stood. At least some of her concern was directed towards his hand, he realised, which was clamped to his chest, still throbbing from Jardine's pincer grip. Spike forced himself to release it. 'There's a meeting tomorrow with the consultant,' he said. 'I promised Peter's sister I'd go through his belongings in advance.' He paused. 'Just in case.'

The nurse gave a nod, then picked up a key card and hung it around her neck. 'Just don't terrorise any more of our patients, OK?'

Spike waited until she was gone, then stepped into the ward. Peter was still the only patient; Spike gave his prostrate form a nod, then knelt down by his bed, checking for a cardboard box or suitcase. Nothing but a softening butter sachet coated in dust. He dropped it in the bin marked 'Clinical Waste' then drew up a chair.

The bandage on Peter's head had been removed, revealing a mustard-coloured bruise on his brow with a deep black cut in the centre, held together by three ugly surgical stitches. His beard had thickened and his body seemed to take up less space on the bed. Spike glanced at the wheeled sideboard and saw the flowers he'd brought on his last visit still languishing. 'Something's going on, Pete,' he said. 'Something to do with Simon Grainger.' Galliano was looking away; Spike reached over and gently rolled his face towards him. His left eye was weeping, welded closed, but the right was open a fraction, lids trembling slightly.

'Pete?' Spike said, hearing his voice rise in expectation. He caught a sourness to his friend's breath as he leaned in. Was that a good sign? Then his eyelids stilled, and Spike realised it was probably just a dream, or some automatic reflex.

Sitting back, Spike lowered his head into his hands and thought out loud. 'Did Simon Grainger tell you he'd found the *Flos Sanctus Montis*? Did he want to salvage the wreck without cutting in Neptune?' The grind of Galliano's ventilator was worse than silence. 'Did Jardine know something? Did he come to the office with a bottle of rum?'

A noise came from behind. 'I said talk *to* him, not at him,' the nurse called out with a sympathetic smile. Hooked over her shoulder was a bulky white plastic bag marked GHA – Gibraltar Health Authority.

Spike stood and took the bag. 'May I have a bit of time in private with him?'

The nurse looked a little hurt. 'There's a form you need to fill in if you want to take that away.'

'Understood. Thank you.'

Alone again, Spike swung the bag onto the adjacent bed. A brown paper tag with Galliano's name, hospital number and admission date was attached to its string handle. Spike emptied out the contents: stiff black brogues, scuffed with mud; suit trousers, vast around the waist; jacket and a tent-sized white shirt with dried blood on the breast. Something hard lay in the corner of the bag: Spike pulled out a clear zip-loc baggie containing a phone, wallet, keys, two packs of ultralight cigarettes, half a tube of Extra Strong Mints . . . He tried the phone but the battery was dead. No briefcase. Saddened by the faint aroma of Peter's cologne, he began carefully to fold up the clothes. As he smoothed down the jacket, he felt something crinkle beneath the cotton. He smiled: only Peter was a large enough man to carry an entire document in his inside pocket. Reaching inside, he drew out a white A4 envelope. Seeing the crest of the Garrison Library on the front, he felt something flutter in his stomach, something he hadn't felt in a while. Hope, maybe. He slid out a stapled document, a thin facsimile copy of a ledger table. At the top, in italic writing, was a date – 11th February 1736 – and a title beside it, *El Manifiesto del Barco 'Flos Sanctus Montis'*.

Chapter Thirty-nine

Spike carried the ship's manifest towards the window. The glow that emanated from the smokers' courtyard was brighter than the halogen bulb on the ceiling. The Spanish text was still almost impossible to decipher. Either the facsimile was out of focus – it looked to have been made at the very advent of the technology – or the original manifest had been blurred. Either way, Spike spent too long trying to establish the principal goods on board, only to discover that he was actually looking at the ship's departure point, Montevideo – in present-day Uruguay presumably – and intended destination, Málaga.

The ledger had a number of early entries that Spike couldn't understand, but he started to feel more at ease when he translated a line confirming the presence of forty-two carcasses of *lomo saltado* – salted beef. Evidently the *Holy Flower of the Mountain* had been a fairly substantial vessel.

A few more mysterious entries, then a final one that caught his eye, mostly because he'd heard the phrase so recently. '*Pesos de ocho*'. He switched his fingertip to the column marked 'Quantity'. The number was clear – 42,300. 'Forty-two thousand, three hundred pieces of eight,' he said aloud. 'Bloody hell.'

Spike thought about the ship's bell sitting in Amy's cupboard and the old bronze coin beside it. Wherever Simon Grainger had found that bell, thousands of other coins were likely to be lying nearby.

He took out his phone and called her landline. No reply: probably putting Charlie down, or whatever the phrase was. On a whim, he tried her husband's mobile. No such number – probate had finally closed down the account.

As he pocketed his phone, he turned and saw that Peter was facing him now, eyes still closed, mouth agape. Spike had been sitting on the other side of the bed before and had eased Peter's head towards him. How could he be looking now in the opposite direction?

He stepped towards the prone body of his friend, then heard footsteps outside and called out, 'I think he just moved!' Just before the nurse appeared, he grabbed the plastic bag and slipped the manifest inside.

The nurse glanced from Spike to the possessions still laid out on the bed. 'Are you sure?'

'Can you get the doctor?'

'What about all that stuff?'

'Everything's accounted for . . . I'll be back tomorrow.'

Plastic bag in hand, Spike strode past the nurse for the door, unable, for a moment, to keep the smile from his face.

Chapter Forty

The levanter was really blowing now, sweeping in from the east, its passage over the Mediterranean gobbling up billions of drops of warm water to exhale vaporously over the Rock. Window frames shook, palm fronds crackled, the locals barricaded themselves into their houses for the night. Of the apes which had been strutting around town earlier there was no sign.

Head lowered, Spike battled his way into Upper Castle Gulley, seeing the mist rolling ominously down the foothills of the Rock. With Peter's plastic hospital bag flapping violently in the wind, he stopped to check his phone and was reassured to find no new messages. A deflated beach football blew out of the sports cage of Keightley House; he punted it back inside, then shouldered open the door to Block C, feeling a sense of relief as it slammed closed behind him.

The ground-floor lights hummed. Spike checked Amy's pigeonhole and found it empty. She must be at home, at least.

There was no noise from the flats he passed, just the wind wailing outside as moonlight flickered through the landing windows, casting shadows over the wall tiles of the occupants' favoured saints.

On the sixth floor, Spike paused to look out of the broken window. Beneath O'Hara's Battery, the wind was toying with the Rock scrub, flattening its foliage like an animal's fur. As he climbed to the top floor, he felt something give beneath his foot. He looked down and saw the upturned sole of a slipper. The soft-toy snout of a monkey grinned up.

'Amy?' Spike called up the stairs.

He edged to the open stairwell and peered up. The lights were all off. He was about to continue his climb, when he saw something move above him, then heard a slow, deep creak.

'Charlie?' he shouted, feeling a wave of anxiety for the boy which surprised him.

The movement came again, swaying through the empty space, silent and ghostly, like a barn owl changing perch.

'Who's there?'

Eyes still drawn upwards, Spike moved rapidly up the stairs. Out on the Rock, a more powerful burst of wind shrieked through the jagged crags. As the noise faded, Spike heard the creak again, like a ship's mooring under stress. He rounded the corner to the last flight of stairs, fear tightening his chest. A yard in front, suspended at chest height, dangled a pale, naked foot. Swinging beside it was a slipper. Spike stopped, puzzled, then lifted his eyes higher and saw Amy Grainger hanging by her neck from the top-floor banisters.

He blinked, trying to take in what he was seeing. Amy wore the same stripy T-shirt and tracksuit bottoms as the night before last. Tight beneath her chin was a noose of thick yellow rope.

Rushing forward, Spike reached up to grab her legs. He tried to push her up from below, but failed to get a purchase. Her other slipper fell, tumbling down the gap in the stairwell and alighting delicately on the lower landing.

Spike focused on breathing as he tried to think, then forced himself to let go of her legs, sickened to feel the weight return to her neck. Sprinting up the last flight of stairs, he slid over the lino on his knees and pushed his arms painfully through the banisters to hook her shoulders from above. He heaved upwards, noticing a small red welt on the side of her neck, seeing the dream he'd had about Zahra flash before his eyes as he mustered all his strength and pulled. He was just about holding her weight when he saw her head loll forward feebly in its noose. 'Help!' he called out. 'Please! Somebody help me.'

Arms trembling uncontrollably, he inched his mouth towards her small delicate face. 'It's OK,' he whispered into her ear. 'I've got you.'

His knees were sliding forward, so he shifted position, seeing her neck tip to the side, chin at a strange angle. Her eyes were half open; he felt an unbearable need to close them. 'Help!' he yelled again, then heard a door open below as a large man in a grimy vest peered up the stairwell.

'Jesus God!' Spike heard as the man vanished around the flight of stairs. Slow breaths, then heavy footsteps, and Spike was aware of someone standing above him. 'Come in behind me,' he said, catching a smell of crisps and old sweat. 'Grab her shoulders.' He felt soft flabby arms pressing over him, clasping Amy's shoulders; now they were both heaving her upwards, rolling her legs over the banisters, chin still slumped to her collarbone, noose finally slack enough for Spike to lift it over her head.

They laid her carefully down on the landing floor. 'Call an ambulance,' Spike said to the man, then knelt beside Amy, placing his mouth on the same lips he'd kissed just forty-eight hours before. He blew in and out, pressing her chest with his hands. Above, he heard the fat man talking rapidly in *yanito* to an operator. Spike kept going for a long time after he'd realised it was over, then sat back on his heels, eyes stinging. It was then that he noticed that the front door to the Graingers' flat was open.

Chapter Forty-one

'Charlie?'

The lights in the flat were out; Spike flicked them on one by one, frantically looking for the baby monitor. It sat on the kitchen table, the LED green, a tinny rendition of a nursery rhyme emanating eerily from the speakers.

He ran from the kitchenette to the hall, stopping by a white door with 'Charlie's Room' marked in uneven multicoloured stickers on the front. He pushed it open. The cot was empty, a bedraggled toy rabbit propped against the bars.

Back on the landing, the fat man was kneeling over Amy's body, palms pressed together in prayer. Spike grabbed Peter's hospital bag. 'How long did they say?'

'Three minutes,' the man replied.

He returned to the flat and gave one last cry, 'Charlie?', then stopped, drained and hopeless. Wrenching open the storage cupboard, he saw that the coil of ship's rope was missing. The coin and bell were still on the shelf; he hesitated, then swept them into his bag, placing the envelope containing the ship's manifest on top. Voices now, urgent shouting from the stairs.

The first paramedic appeared on the landing, dropping to his knees then testing Amy's pulse. Her face was almost blue. Spike took a step backwards and checked his phone. No new messages. When he looked back up, DS Jessica Navarro was standing in front of him.

Chapter Forty-two

'The boy's missing. Amy's son, Charlie. You've got to find him.'

Spike took in the long black eyelashes and buff physique of Jessica's senior officer, Inspector George Isola. He seemed to take an age to jot Spike's words down, forming the letters in a conscientious childish hand. Spike felt frustration threaten to overwhelm him.

'Perhaps he's with the father,' Isola said.

'The father's dead.'

'Staying with friends?'

'He's two-and-a-half, Inspector. You need to get out there and start looking for him.'

Isola lowered his pad. 'How did you know Mrs Grainger?'

'She was my client. I'm a lawyer.'

'And how did you come to be at your client's flat this evening?'

'I wanted to see her.'

'At 8 p.m.?'

'We were . . .' Spike broke off as Jessica ran back up the stairs, having completed her interview of the fat man.

'You were?' Isola parroted.

'Involved.'

Spike saw Jessica's neck stiffen within the white collar of her police shirt. Isola snapped closed his pad. 'We'll need you to come with us to New Mole House to make a formal statement.'

A third policeman emerged from the flat, holding what looked like a hand-written note between rubber-gloved fingers. He beckoned to

Isola, who turned away, leaving Jessica glaring up at Spike from beneath her chequered hat. 'What's in the bag?' she said, not bothering to keep the contempt from her voice.

Spike pulled open the white bag and showed her the A4 envelope containing the manifest on top. 'Peter's stuff from the hospital.'

'What a prince.' Jessica shook her head, then spoke in an undertone. 'You can't have Zahra. You fuck things up with me. So you sleep with Amy Grainger instead.'

Spike stood there in silence, taking his punishment.

'She was vulnerable, Spike. She'd just lost her husband. And she was your client. Your responsibility.'

Isola returned, issuing orders, motioning for Spike to follow. 'Make sure you sweep the flat for prints,' Spike said as he joined him on the stairs. 'And for fuck's sake start looking for the boy.'

Chapter Forty-three

On his way back from the police station, Spike stopped at the Royal Calpe and bought a packet of cigarettes from the machine by the bar. Two pounds fifty. Cheap smokes – still the bedrock of Gibraltar's economy. Once in the Upper Town, he leant against a damp stucco wall and lit up. The white stick slotted neatly between his fingers as the dry smoke filled his lungs; it was as though he'd never stopped. Even after ten years, there was something intrinsically disappointing about a cigarette: the nicotine never quite seemed to hit the spot. He took a deeper drag and continued walking.

Amy had been confirmed dead, he'd learnt after giving his statement. Charlie was still missing. The child's relatives and friends' parents were being woken one by one as the entire Moorish Castle Estate was meticulously searched. The Chief Constable's assumption was that Charlie had found his mother's body and fled in panic into Gibraltar. Spike wasn't so sure. He knew that a boy would want to stay with his mother, dead or not.

He checked his phone. Still no messages. His head began to spin, either from the nicotine or the growing awareness that he'd been the cause of another death. Charlie might be dead too, or hiding somewhere on the Rock, terrified, alone. Spike had never cared much for children, always finding something alarming in the noise, the mess, the unpredictability. But this solemn boy with his watchful eyes had found a soft spot he'd never known was there. The idea that Spike had put him in danger was almost too much to bear.

As he reached Chicardo's Passage, he could tell at once that something was wrong. Ahead, one of his father's pot plants lay smashed on the cobbles, red geraniums caked with earth. The levanter had been high this evening, but not that high.

He ran for the front door. The wood around the Chubb lock had been splintered and the frame opened with the slightest push.

'Dad?' he shouted as he burst inside to find his father sitting at the kitchen table. Relief was tempered by déjà vu as he recognised the same look on his father's face, the same broken posture, as he'd seen on another terrible night. 'Are you hurt?' he asked, taking in the debris on the floor: dresser overturned, tea chests rummaged through, brown paper bag of Christmas decorations emptied, baubles smashed. 'Dad? Are you hurt?'

Slowly Rufus turned his head, the rims of his eyes pink behind his glasses. 'You were right, son. As usual.'

Spike reached out to touch his father's face. 'What happened, Dad?'

'I came back . . .' Rufus broke off, shaking his head.

Spike waited for him to continue, feeling annoyance rise, even now. 'You came back . . .'

'From Cousin Sandra's. She rang me yesterday. Asked me out to dinner. I thought why not. But when I came back . . .' He stopped again.

'What?'

Rufus's eyes wandered over the chaos of the kitchen.

'Who did it?'

He sighed. 'I didn't see their faces.'

'Whose faces?'

'The burglars. The men you've been warning me about. I didn't bother locking the door tonight, and now this.'

'You said "them"?'

'There were several voices. They must have heard me. Got out onto the balcony and climbed down the front of the house.'

'Did they take anything?'

'I don't know. But look what they've done to your mother's things.'

Hearing his father's breathing grow laboured, Spike took a pack of beta-blockers from the windowsill and stood over him as he swallowed them down like an obedient child. 'I don't want you staying here, Dad,' he said.

'But where can I go?'

'To a hotel? A friend?'

Rufus shook his head.

'Why don't you stay with Cousin Sandra?'

'She was a bit annoying, actually. Could hardly understand what she was saying.' He laughed strangely, and Spike wondered not for the first time how far away they were from adding dementia to his list of ailments. 'How about next door? The Montegriffos have a spare room.'

Rufus nodded, and Spike immediately pushed through the bead curtain up the stairs, finding his bedroom cupboards yanked open, one door pulled from its hinges, clothes unworn for perhaps a decade ripped from hangers and trampled to the ground. The luggage he kept under the bed now lay in the middle of the room, lids unzipped, stained linings ripped. He grabbed the bag he'd taken to Genoa, then moved into Rufus's room, filling it with clothes and medicaments, most of which were strewn over the floor. The bedroom window was half open, he saw, a pot plant smashed and upended on the balcony. Spike jammed the window closed, fingers shaking, from the break-in or Amy's death, he couldn't tell. When he returned downstairs, he found Rufus on his knees, stuffing old papers into one of the tea chests.

'Dad, please. I'll do all that.'

His father put down a sheaf of paper, but remained kneeling, eyes fixed on the cork-tile floor. 'You were right about another thing, son. I did let your mother down. I let her down terribly.'

'Come on, Dad. We don't need to do this now.'

'"J" is for Juliet. Your sister.'

Spike stood stock-still, foolishly clutching his father's suitcase.

'She was stillborn, you see. You were three years old.' There was a pause as Rufus struggled to find the words. 'Your mother went mad with grief. The doctors told her to write it down. Hoped it might help her to get it off her chest.' He removed his glasses and looked up at Spike, eyes raw. 'We tried for another child but it never happened. That's when she started drinking. I wasn't strong enough to help her.'

Tears began to slide down Rufus's lined face. 'She's buried in the North Front Cemetery, son. Close to your mother.'

Spike crouched beside him. 'It's OK, Dad. I know you did your best.'

Carefully, Spike helped his father up, then led him outside onto the street. The budgie flapped and cheeped as the neighbouring door opened. Keith Montegriffo wore paisley pyjamas as his wife peered down behind him from the staircase, unrecognisable in hair-rollers and an old cotton nightdress.

'There's been a break-in,' Spike said. 'I wondered if Dad could stay with you.'

'My God, Rufus,' Mr Montegriffo replied, widening the door. 'Are you hurt? Come in! Come in!'

'I told you, Keith,' Spike heard from the stairs, 'I warned you. It's those tinkermen. They're not here just selling bangles, you know.'

'It wasn't a tinker I heard,' Rufus said as he marched inside, folding his tweed jacket onto the hallway table. 'It was a Scotsman.'

Spike turned from the door. 'What did you say?'

'A Scottish accent. Clear as daylight.' Rufus stared at Spike, then tapped the hearing aid in the frame of his glasses. 'First thing I did when I came home was turn this up. And there he was upstairs, yammering away to his pal. Och aye this, och aye that.'

Spike thanked the Montegriffos and closed the door behind him.

Chapter Forty-four

Back home, Spike took the bell and the coin from the hospital bag and placed them next to each other on the kitchen table. Kneeling amid the mess of spilt bags of sugar and spice jars on the floor, he found an unbroken bottle of white-wine vinegar, which he tipped onto a tea towel. Massaging the coin with a rag-clad finger brought away a layer of bluish grime. He repeated the motion until the towel was dotted with stains. Resisting the temptation to run the coin under the tap, he poured neat vinegar over it, then wrapped it in the tea towel and rubbed it vigorously between his palms. When he took it out, one edge had crumbled. The rest was gleaming: he held it to the light and found glinting silver metal.

He took out his phone and ran through the list of recently dialled numbers. Cádiz prefix . . . '*Hola?*' came a brusque female voice.

'*Puedo hablar con Juan?*'

'*Es tarde.*'

'*Es emergencia.*'

The woman muttered something to someone beside her, a disgruntled husband presumably. There followed the creak of a door and a shrill cry, '*Juan-i-to?*'

Another extension picked up as Juan's mother slammed the phone down.

'It's Spike Sanguinetti.'

Spike heard a small sigh of disappointment. 'What do you want?'

'I need to ask you something.'

'I was asleep.'

'I'll be quick. Can silver get bronze disease?'

On the other end of the line, Spike sensed Juan's professional vanity doing battle with his dislike. 'Yes and no . . .' he said eventually.

'Meaning?'

'The metal might look like it has bronze disease. But it's more likely to be verdigris.'

'Verdi-what?'

'What are we talking about here? A coin?'

'Yes.'

'Well, pure silver is too soft to be made into anything practical. So it's usually alloyed with more hardy metals. Copper, mainly. Which makes it susceptible to verdigris. A mild bronze disease that doesn't ruin the artefact. What type of coin?'

'*Un peso de ocho.*'

'Same era as the bell?'

'I think so.'

'Well, *pesos* were made of sterling silver. Eight *reales'* worth, in fact – hence, "pieces of eight". Over ninety per cent pure, a new international standard for the time. You'll probably find the discoloration is just skin deep. A patina caused by age. Particularly if it's been lying on the seabed near other metals. With slow and conscientious cleaning the surface dirt will come away.'

Spike glanced down at his filthy tea towel.

'Do you have more work for me?' Juan said.

'Not at the moment.'

Juan cleared his throat. 'I don't suppose you could give me the phone number of that girl you were with?'

Spike almost laughed. '*Hasta luego*, Juan. She's out of your league.' And mine, he admitted to himself. 'When the recession's over, I suggest you return to the museum and ask for your old job back.'

Spike hung up and re-examined the coin. Stamped on one side was an image of the Pillars of Hercules, the phrase 'plus ultra' written below. The Romans had thought there was nowhere to go beyond Gibraltar, but the Spanish had proven otherwise. On the flip side was a crest, the number 8 beside it. So *pesos de ocho* were silver, not bronze. The *Holy Flower of the Mountain* had been carrying silver.

Up on his feet, Spike reached above the kitchen units: at least the bastards had left him the whisky. He poured himself a glass and sat back, thinking hard. Could Neptune have discovered a cache of Spanish coins lying on the seabed near the lead they were extracting? If so, they wouldn't have had a right to them – sovereign coins were the automatic property of the country that issued them. Neptune wouldn't have been able to sell the coins on the open market, so they'd come up with a neat solution. Invented a story that the *Gloucester* was smuggling silver – in untraceable, unmarked bars. All they then had to do was salvage the coins on the quiet, melt them down, and then they could sell the silver legitimately. Spike reached for his packet of Bensons. What if Simon Grainger had seen Neptune's boat working in the Straits? He'd dived the Europa Reef and was familiar with the local wrecks. He knew he'd found a ship's bell close to a site that didn't correspond to a freighter from the Crimean War. Maybe the crew had dined at Grainger's restaurant and he'd mentioned something to one of them, causing Clohessy to panic. Grainger was in a position to expose Neptune's criminality. The salvage had been valued at twenty-four million pounds. A prize worth killing for . . .

Spike heard a bang, and shot to his feet, but it was just the levanter, blowing closed the broken door frame. Grabbing a chair from the kitchen, he propped it beneath the handle. He couldn't stay here tonight, he realised. Just then, he felt a sensation in his pocket that made his stomach lurch. A small, persistent vibration.

Sender: Enrico Sanguinetti. Another message from a ghost. *I have the boy. Meet me at 10 p.m. tomorrow by Europa Point Lighthouse. The child in exchange for the phone. Tell the police and I will kill him.*

Spike shut his eyes, feeling disgust sweep through his body, horrified by the damage that his digging and interference had caused. He tried to light a cigarette but his hand was shaking. It was time to go to the police. This was too much to handle alone.

He looked again at the text message. *Tell the police and I will kill him.* How could anyone have known about his relationship with Amy and Charlie? Had they tapped his phone? Were they tracing his calls? His texts? He could still go to Jessica for help. But what if they had a contact in the police force, or access to police frequencies?

He poured himself another glass, and then another. Time passed, and when he next looked down, he found that half the cigarettes were gone, and that an idea was starting to take shape. It was messy. Risky and wholly likely to fail, but it was the germ of a plan. He suddenly felt strangely calm.

Throwing some clothes into a bag, he swung open his broken front door and walked out into the street. Inside the phone box on the corner, he watched his fingers hesitate on the push keys. But before he had time to change his mind, he had dialled Clohessy's number.

It went to voicemail so he left a message – he was learning how effective they could be. 'I've got the ship's bell. I want two kilos of the silver. Meet me tomorrow at Europa Point Lighthouse. 10.15 p.m.'

Placing the greasy black receiver back in its cradle, he stared out through the mullioned windows into the darkness. Now there was no way back.

*

Complicated? Manda huevos! That is an understatement. Grabbing the child proves easy enough. He doesn't struggle as I press the gun to his temple, waiting for his mother to write her own suicide note with a trembling hand. A bit of mewling as I tape up his wrists, catching the mother with a truncheon blow to the neck as she surges towards me with surprising courage, apparently undeterred by the gun. He only goes completely quiet when I tape up his eyes, like a bird with its cage covered. So far, so straightforward, but then – Dios! Getting him downstairs, his little feet kicking, crying out for his mother who is swinging now from the spindles, so that I have to cover his hot little mouth with my hand, milk teeth nipping at my palm.

The SEAT is parked outside the tower block. I cover him with a blanket and shove him into the boot, driving around for a while until I find a quieter place. And there it is – a lighthouse. Striped, windswept, the ends of the earth.

Once I'm sure that no one else is around, I roll down the front windows a slit, then reach into the back and shunt forward one of the rear seats. Through the gap, I make out the sound of rapid, muffled breathing. Opening the boot, I reel at the smell and see a stain at the base of the boy's vest where he has fouled himself. He is sleeping now, perhaps lulled by the motion. I take a sports-cap bottle of water from the glove compartment and slip the teat into his mouth. When half the bottle is gone, I withdraw it and rip off his blindfold. He starts to cry, but not as much as when I pull the gun from my waistband. I show it to him, and his eyes widen. 'If you kick,' I say in English, 'if you scream or make a noise, I will go back for your mother. Your mama. You understand?' The boy stares at the gun, mute. 'You understand me, boy?' He nods, and I let him have the rest of the bottle, which he sucks down greedily, water spilling down his dimpled chin.

I slam the boot, then drive to the multi-storey car park I have scouted near the hotel, choosing a deserted corner on the top floor. The boy is sleeping again; I chuck in another bottle of water, then set off down the stairs, avoiding the CCTV cameras, feeling the film of sweat on my forehead drying in the cool, ventilated air.

Back in my hotel room, with the soft strains of a classical guitar settling my mind, I send a text with the instructions for tomorrow. Sleep feels easy and close: I shut my eyes and wait for tomorrow.

Chapter Forty-five

Spike awoke in a single room on the second floor of the Cannon Hotel. He'd stayed here a few times before, back in the days when he and Drew Stanford-Trench had made a game of picking up tourists in town. Spike had proved surprisingly successful – play the Latin angle with the British girls, work the British accent with everyone else. The small functional rooms hadn't changed much. Perhaps that was why they were almost always available – even at 11.30 p.m., the time Spike had turned up last night.

It was early now, he could tell as he glanced at the window, the sun still hiding behind the Rock. He realised why he'd woken: guitar music was streaming through the thin wall of the adjoining room. Irritatingly jaunty – Rodrigo, it sounded like. A vindictive Spaniard, perhaps, fantasising about a red and gold flag flying from the Rock.

Spike tried to go back to sleep, but images of Amy's suspended body began to rush through his mind. Then of Charlie, held captive, dangled like bait to lure Spike and his phone. Focus on the boy, he told himself as he slid out of bed. That was all that mattered now.

Wrapping himself in the tiny hotel towel, he paced the corridor to the shared bathroom. The flow of water, though pitiful, helped to clear his mind, and last night's drunken plan began to take a clearer shape. There were things to be done today, tasks to be achieved.

Back in his bedroom, the music stopped as his neighbour slammed his own door and headed for the shower. Spike scoured the room for somewhere to stash the ship's bell, settled on the top of the cupboard, then went downstairs to breakfast, hangover mounting with each step.

The owner and her elderly mother were conferring on the ground-floor patio, scrutinising a flier.

'Have you heard?' the mother whispered as she passed Spike a leaflet. The upper section was marked 'RGP' – Royal Gibraltar Police.

'A boy's gone missing,' she said. 'Little Charlie Grainger. First his father, now his mum. Poor sweet *chuni*.'

Spike stared down at the photocopied image of a younger, happier Charlie, recognising it with a pang as one which had sat in a frame on the sideboard of Amy's flat.

'They've closed the border,' the owner said. 'All flights grounded until they find him. People are meeting in Casemates Square at 10 a.m. to help with the search.'

Spike thanked them and went through to the dining room. Only one other table was occupied, a reminder of the challenge of running a hotel in a booming economy when cheaper accommodation could be found on the opposite side of the border. His fellow diner was an ageing British skinhead in a singlet and shorts. Curled in the middle of his adjacent place setting was a silver necklace, perhaps belonging to someone he had once come here with.

The owner brought in a plate of brittle bacon, fried eggs and wrinkled sausages. Spike pushed it aside, downed his doll-size tumbler of reconstituted orange juice, then went outside, recoiling from the hazy glare of the early morning.

The atmosphere in town felt immediately different, clusters of concerned locals standing on street corners, handing out leaflets, policemen in fluorescent waistcoats lining Main Street. The skies were quiet, the occasional cackle of a herring gull intermingling with the throaty roar of patrol boats out in the Straits.

Spike hurried to Chambers via the backstreets, glancing in at ground-floor windows and seeing pensioners watching GBC News in their front rooms. Once in his office, he locked the door and opened his laptop. It took him slightly more than an hour to compose a document entitled 'The Conduct of Neptune Marine and the Salvage of the *Gloucester*'. While it printed, he followed up on a question which had occurred to him late into his restless night. He was certain that he remembered a boozy evening when Galliano had spoken of the illicit nature of ivory. It turned out, as it usually did, that Peter had been right. A Google search revealed that the UK was a signatory to the Convention on International Trade in Endangered Species. And if the UK was, that meant Gibraltar was too – while local government dealt with internal issues, matters of foreign policy and defence were still dictated by Whitehall. Under the terms of the Convention, it was illegal to raise even the smallest amount of ivory from the sea floor. The fork that Clohessy had shown to Spike aboard the *Trident* might have seemed innocuous, but it still meant that his company had broken the Convention. Technically, Neptune must halt salvage until the ivory had been returned to its resting place in the sea.

Spike marked the relevant pages of the Convention with a Post-it note and placed them, along with copies of his own document and the manifest of the *Flos Sanctus Montis*, in an envelope addressed to Drew Stanford-Trench. Whatever happened to Spike tonight, at least opposing counsel would have all the information he needed. At the last moment, Spike wrapped the silver *peso de ocho* in a tissue and slipped it inside. Then he grabbed his phone and braced himself for what lay ahead.

Chapter Forty-six

Rocky's Pictures in the ICC Mall was open, a lone tourist printing out repetitive photos of the Barbary Apes, perhaps wondering why the centre of town was so quiet. Haresh, the shopkeeper, looked grimly resigned to the lack of business.

Spike lingered by a display cabinet of cheap frames and T-shirts emblazoned with catalogue images of laughing children until the shop was empty.

'Not going to Casemates?' Haresh asked. Despite the fact that his family had settled on the Rock soon after India's independence, he still spoke with a strong Rajasthan accent.

'Maybe later,' Spike said.

There was a pause, then Spike cleared his throat. 'Listen, Haresh. I need a favour . . .'

Haresh's frown deepened as Spike explained what he wanted.

'So you do not want me to send the pictures from your phone to my computer,' Haresh repeated back slowly.

'Under no circumstances.'

'And I must place your phone screen on the scanner and physically capture the images that way.'

'Then save them on a disc.'

Haresh held out his pink-lined palm, and Spike opened the first picture message and handed it to him, catching a glimpse of Žigon's shrewd confident eyes on the phone screen. As Haresh placed the device on the scanner, Spike snapped, 'Careful,' and he lowered the lid more delicately. The photocopier emitted a flash of light, then the blurry image of a man in a hotel corridor appeared on the monitor above.

'Can't you make it any clearer?' Spike said.

'I'll touch it up later,' Haresh replied defensively as he handed back Spike back his phone. 'Next.'

'This one's from Halloween.'

'In August?'

Haresh peered down at the gruesome image of Enrico's body. Through the shop window, Spike saw a group of locals hurrying by, presumably joining in the search for Charlie. He turned back to Haresh, reminded again of the urgency. 'How long will it take to clean them up?'

'Should be done by this afternoon.'

Spike gave Haresh a nod, then put his phone back into his pocket and left.

Chapter Forty-seven

The nurses' station was empty, the swing doors to the ward propped open, hushed voices audible within. Spike moved towards the entrance and saw a group of people gathered around Peter Galliano's bed. On the near side was the bird-like form of Hilary Silva, as lean as Peter had been fat, blue mascara blurred as she held her brother's hand. Crouching beside her was the nurse Spike knew, while two doctors in hospital scrubs stood on the far side of the bed, one peering at Peter's chart, the other checking his ventilator.

Hilary turned her head as Spike entered the ward. She looked confused, overwhelmed even, and Spike suddenly wished he was anywhere but there. But a moment later, her lips tightened into a smile. Spike glanced at the nurse and saw that she was smiling too.

'I asked Peter to squeeze my hand,' Hilary Silva croaked as Spike approached. 'And he did it, Spike. He squeezed my hand.'

A moment later, Spike found himself embracing her so hard he was worried she might crack. One of the doctors came round to their side of the bed. 'We don't want to crowd him,' she said to Spike briskly.

Spike nodded, smiling as he saw that Galliano's eyes were half open, irises roving, drool spilling from his mouth, lacquering his beard. He bent down and whispered in his ear: 'I'm going to sort things out, Pete. I'm not quite sure how, but I will.'

Galliano stared back at him. Then all of a sudden he gave a wink, and Spike felt his smile broaden. 'Amazing,' he murmured as the doctor steered him back to the door. 'Just amazing.'

She herded him past the desk. 'I've already explained this to Peter's sister, Mr Sanguinetti,' she said evenly. 'You need to remember that it's very early days. We still don't know how serious the brain injury is. These are encouraging signs, but no more than that.'

Spike nodded, aware that he was grinning like an imbecile.

'He needs to rest now; you can come back this evening.'

'Tomorrow,' Spike said. 'Hopefully I'll be back tomorrow.'

Chapter Forty-eight

The silence of the skies was broken as Spike emerged from the hospital to find a police helicopter hovering over the western flank of the Rock. The sense of elation he'd felt at Peter's bedside vanished. His phone began to ring: it was Jessica. 'Any news?' Spike asked.

'Not yet. But we're doing everything we can.'

The background noise was oppressive: Spike could barely hear her. 'Where are you?' he shouted.

'In a boat. Checking the coves around Catalan Bay.'

He heard a man's voice shouting orders above the engine of the speedboat: 'Gorgeous' George Isola, no doubt.

'Is there anything else you can tell us?' Jessica said to Spike. 'Something you might have forgotten?'

Spike hesitated for a moment. *Tell the police and I will kill him.* 'No, nothing else,' he replied, then almost changed his mind before realising that she'd already hung up. As he came into Casemates, he saw that half the restaurants and cafés had their grilles lowered: most of the catering staff were Spanish, and a closed border left no one to flip burgers or wait tables. The only movement was a house sparrow enjoying a dust bath beneath a eucalyptus tree. The hushed atmosphere stirred memories of when Franco had shut the frontier, sealing the Gibraltarians inside, helping them to forge their proud yet adaptable nature.

Midway through the square, Spike paused to watch the tail end of a crowd climbing Demayas Ramp. The road was crammed with people – schoolkids marshalled by teachers, men and women in suits, Arabs, Jews, Hindus, Christians, all united in the search for a stolen child. Spike felt a momentary glow of pride, until he remembered that he was the reason for this show of solidarity.

At least the 'All's Well' pub was open; he sat down on the terrace, receiving a glare from the Liverpudlian waiter, annoyed to have his viewing of a pre-season football match interrupted. Checking the time – still an hour before the photographs would be ready – he took the faded airmail letter from the pocket of his cargo trousers and carefully unfolded it.

'My darling J,' Spike read. 'I still can't sleep, so I've left your father to snore alone. I don't think he'll even notice I'm gone. I'm sitting on the balcony of our holiday apartment, sipping the rough Burgundy from supper, watching the tide roll onto the shore. S wears himself out during the hot days here – building huge sandcastles with R on the beach below, tearing himself away from the water long enough only to beg for ice cream. So he does not stir in bed, a mercy on nights when I feel like this, when the pain of losing you is so raw. People think it strange to grieve so long for a child who never lived. But they are wrong. You did live. Inside me. I also mourn for the life we might have had together. The memories we might have made which have been stolen from us. R wants to move on, to live. It is his nature. I know that he loves me, but he does not know how to make things better, and that hurts him dreadfully. He is a man who needs to fix things, to solve problems, but I think that we are both beginning to realise that he cannot fix me . . .'

Spike closed the letter. He'd never really thought about how it might feel to lose a child. How it could destroy a person. At least Amy had never suffered the pain of knowing that her son was missing. That was something, wasn't it? Leaving a stack of coins for his drink, he continued on foot towards Devil's Tower Road, aware that there was another stop he needed to make.

Chapter Forty-nine

The North Front Cemetery was the only graveyard in Gibraltar still in use, the others having reached bursting point last century. It grew larger by the year, though its indefinite expansion was checked by the airport runway which ran along the far side. At least the planes were silent today.

Inside, Spike saw thousands of headstones huddled together, sun-bleached and upright, contrasting with the older, crooked graves of the Trafalgar Cemetery, where the injured had been buried from the famous naval battle which had taken place twenty miles off the coast of Gib. Spike moved towards the middle row, passing the section for the unconsecrated dead, feeling his feet sink into the soft pathways – the cemetery was built on the narrow sandy isthmus that connected Gibraltar to Spain, always a boon for gravediggers. Finally he reached the simple white marble of his mother's headstone. A vase was pegged into the earth beside it, the glass smudged and dirty. He plucked it from its ring and polished it on his T-shirt, realising that once again he had failed to bring flowers. Not that it mattered – she was dead and gone and no God was smiling down on those who remembered her. He squinted through the sunlight at the inscription: '*Catherine Rose Sanguinetti, beloved wife of Rufus, mother of Somerset, missed beyond all bearing*'. 'Why didn't you just *say* something?' he asked aloud. Sensing someone move behind him, he turned to see a hunched old man, hands clasped behind his back. The man gave a nod as if to say, 'We all must carry on . . .'

He stepped over Catherine Sanguinetti's grave and stopped by a smaller granite block two rows in front. '*JS*' the inscription read. '*Born 16/01/1977. Died 16/01/1977. Always in our hearts*'. Juliet. His sister. Born and died on the same day. Spike crouched down and touched the stone. Its darkness had absorbed a little of the sun's heat, and it warmed his palm. Shutting his eyes, he thought of his mother, and of the sister he had never known, of Amy Grainger and Enrico Sanguinetti, both dead, of Charlie and Zahra, both missing. Tears pricked his eyes, until he remembered Žigon's cold lazy-eyed stare, and turned to walk away past his mother's grave, trailing his fingertips over the top of her headstone, feeling his grief harden into a small, tight knot of anger.

Chapter Fifty

Dusk was falling as Spike locked up the office and moved into the evening traffic of Europa Road. Echoing in the distance, he heard the last cries of the search party as they returned to the Moorish Castle Estate, still calling out for Charlie Grainger, knocking on doors, checking abandoned buildings. Some people thought he might have fled up onto the Rock, hoping to find his dead father; Spike had overheard one person suggest that the apes might have taken him. By now, the police would have searched every part of the Upper Rock accessible by foot. On his way back from the graveyard to the photo shop, Spike had made out tiny figures moving inside the gates of the military base, usually forbidden to civilians.

Distrust had been etched on Haresh's brow as he'd handed Spike the disc. When Spike had asked if he could also take the cardboard box marked 'Xerox' lying behind the counter, Haresh had asked to be compensated for each remaining sheet of photographic paper inside. It had been worth it though – the box was just the right size to transport a ship's bell.

Back on Main Street, Spike had slipped the disc into a jiffy bag addressed to his contact at Interpol. By the end of the week an image of Žigon – and of his work – would be safely in the hands of the authorities. And Spike's mobile phone would bear no electronic trace of the photographs having been sent.

Now that the package had been posted, Spike carried nothing but the empty Xerox box past the cable-car station, skirting the gates of the Alameda Gardens, trying not to think of the time he'd spent there with Zahra, nor of the nightmare he'd had about her in Genoa.

It was gone 8.30 p.m. He'd wanted to scout out the location for at least an hour before the handover, but had forgotten how long it took to reach Europa Point on foot. It was a part of Gibraltar he always tried to avoid. To his left rose the Rock, the steps to Jews' Gate winding up its flank, the point above which the search helicopter had hovered this morning. Beside it lay a shrine to the Pillars of Hercules, a plaque explaining how Hercules had torn Africa and Europe in two to celebrate one of his Labours, and how the Romans had believed Gibraltar to mark the gateway to Hell on account of the maze of caves and passages deep within its porous limestone. *Mons Calpe*, Hollow Mountain. Even the most impregnable fortress could have a vulnerable centre.

The levanter was gusting again, the first wisps of cloud appearing on the foothills of the Rock. After a brisk ten-minute walk, Spike rounded a corner and saw the southernmost tip of Gibraltar spread out before him, flat and windswept, a handful of disused military huts scattered over the sand dunes and a squat, red-and-white-striped lighthouse protruding from the edge of the cliffs.

The road curved around a dusty cricket pitch, laid on to entertain the Forces, rarely used these days. Spike remembered watching a match there as a boy, the Army vs. the Navy, hot red-faced Englishmen in whites berating and applauding each other in equal measure, oblivious to the loyal Gibraltarians gathered at the boundary. The only piece of green that now remained was an astroturf wicket in the balding nets.

A bungalow describing itself almost accurately as 'The Last Shop on Earth' stood behind the pitch. It had once sold souvenirs and food, but lack of tourist custom had led to closure. Spike paused by its boarded-up windows, staring out at the Straits and the dark Rif mountains of Morocco breaking the evening haze.

Parked on the road beside the cricket pitch was a bus, optimistically waiting for passengers to board before beginning its route back to town. The last departure was 9.30 p.m.; this, and the complete absence of CCTV on Europa Point, led Spike to conclude that whomever he was due to meet must have done an extensive recce before deciding on the venue.

He passed beneath the lighthouse, a hundred and sixty feet high, its revolving electric warnings automated by Trinity House in London, the only one of its kind outside Britain to enjoy the honour. Beneath it lay a shingle-covered viewing platform; below that was a fifty-foot drop to a cove known as Deadman's Beach. Somehow appropriate, Spike thought, as he crossed the shingle.

Beyond the cricket pitch, the bus driver fired up his engine. Watching the bus drive away through the thickening fog, Spike suddenly felt like the last man left on the continent. Red brake lights vanished into the gloom, and he checked the road again, seeing the steep incline of the Rock above, a track climbing the lower slope towards a dark tunnel mouth, its entrance blocked with steel bars. There were no other vehicles in sight.

He set the empty cardboard box down on the viewing platform, felt the wind threaten it, so picked up a handful of shingle and threw it inside. The box held firm, and again he ran through the plan in his mind, feeling a sudden longing for a drink, a little alarming in its intensity. Instead he lit a cigarette, aware that it might be for the last time. When he looked back up, a small blue car was rolling towards him along the coast road.

Chapter Fifty-one

Spike flicked his cigarette over the cliff edge as the car drew to a stop on the road, headlights slicing through the fog that was drifting steadily now down the Rock. 9.45 p.m.: too early. Clohessy wasn't due to arrive for another half an hour. Whatever slim chance of success Spike's plan had would vanish completely if Clohessy failed to turn up on time.

Slowly Spike held up his mobile phone. The car flashed its lights in recognition, sending a surge of adrenalin into his bloodstream.

He beckoned to the driver to come closer. He needed him here on the viewing platform, as prominent as possible for Clohessy and his men to see. Heart shifting, Spike watched as the car crept forwards, indicating fastidiously before turning onto the viewing platform.

A blue SEAT Ibiza, hatch-backed and flimsy. Could this really constitute a threat? The driver reversed into the space furthest from Spike, boot tight to the low cliff wall behind, the scene briefly lit up by a beam from the lighthouse, which gave a first rotation of warning to the shipping traffic fetching in and out of the Straits behind.

With a soft click, the car door opened and a man stepped out. Before the flash of the lighthouse faded, Spike saw that he was of average height, a slightly bulging stomach covered by a short-sleeved shirt tucked into faded jeans. Then the beam receded and his face was subsumed again by darkness and fog. 'Your phone, please,' the man called out in a lisping, Spanish accent.

The lighthouse gave a second flash, providing Spike with a glimpse of a pair of dull brown spectacles obscuring the man's eyes. Every instinct told Spike that he could take him out, over-power him. But there was too much at risk. 'I want to see the boy,' he called back.

The Spaniard nodded, then began edging around his car, eyes still trained on Spike. Forty years old? Fifty? Again Spike fought the urge to run over and tackle him.

The man pulled open the boot and a dim yellow light ignited within. Spike heard him hiss something in English. Receiving no response, the man jabbed a finger roughly into the space. 'Mama?' came a weak voice, before the boot slammed shut again.

Spike stared across the platform at the nondescript man lean-ing against his shabby car with his paunch and cheap glasses. *You fucking coward*, he thought. 'Well come on then,' he shouted. 'I've got what you want.' He threw his mobile into the cardboard box and shoved it over the shingle with a foot.

'Wait,' the man commanded. 'Stay there.'

The lighthouse rotated again, and for a moment Spike thought he saw a large vehicle moving slowly through the shadows. Clohessy and his team would be driving here from town; given the density of the fog, Spike would surely have seen their head-lamps as they approached, even if they turned them off at the last minute. The beacon flashed again: the road was empty.

Ahead on the viewing platform, the Spaniard had reached his quarry. He crouched down, one hand on the rim of the card-board box, dragging it steadily back towards his car like a jackal with carrion. Opening the passenger door, he took out a laptop and laid it on the roof of the car. As he raised the lid, a bluish light gleamed onto his face, but still the only features Spike could discern were the glasses and a neat fringe of grey hair. He connected a white lead from the computer to Spike's phone, then carefully tapped at the keyboard.

Spike glanced around: most of the road was now entirely hidden by the fog. He could just make out the cricket net, the Rock rising above, the dark mouth of the tunnel disappearing inside it. Waves started to smash against the cliffs behind, and Spike looked back to see an oil tanker powering towards the Atlantic, oblivious of the small drama playing out above it.

The blue light from the car roof extinguished as the man shut the laptop and slid it back through the window of the car. 'Is good,' he called out. 'You do not forward the pictures.'

'I followed your instructions. Just like you told me to. Now let the boy go.'

The man dropped Spike's phone to the ground. Three vicious stamps reduced it to a tangle of crushed plastic and low-alpha lead. When he looked back up, Spike caught a hint of a smile before another cloud of fog rolled in and he became just a disembodied voice. 'OK,' he said. 'Now you take the boy.'

Spike sprinted towards the car boot, almost losing his balance as the backs of his legs pressed to the low cliff wall behind. 'Hurry,' the man called out, waving him on from the road.

A muffled sound came from inside the boot, and Spike thought back to the first time he'd met Charlie Grainger – his chipped silver dinky car grating against a wall. He fumbled with the catch in the dark, then looked up to see the Spaniard standing just a few yards away from him. He reached into the waistband of his trousers and pulled out a small black pistol. 'Message from Žigon,' he called out, a first charge of emotion entering his tone. 'You should not have followed him to Genoa. He does not forget.' Another set of waves began crashing beneath the cliffs. 'The boy's mother . . .' The man was forced to raise his voice to drown out the surf. 'Before she die, she cry for her husband. Not for you.' He took a step forward, and Spike could see that he moved easily now, lithely almost, his shirt flapping freely against his muscular body. 'Tomorrow they find you under the cliff. The boy beside you.' Malice sharpened his voice as he yelled above the breakers,

'You know I meet Žigon's girl one time. And he was right. She is a fucking great whore.'

The Spaniard held out the gun, pointing it at Spike's head. He wore thin black gloves, Spike saw, as he heard the click of what he assumed was a safety catch, and closed his eyes.

Nothing happened. It felt as though time was slowing down, and Spike found himself wondering if this was some strange biological function intended to ease a man's final seconds. But his breaths were still coming, quick and shallow. So he forced himself to open his eyes, and saw that the Spaniard was still pointing the gun at him, but that his face was turned away, forehead wrinkled in puzzlement. His glasses gleamed like coins, and Spike realised that he was being illuminated from behind rather than by the rays of the lighthouse. Where was the light coming from? Spike snapped to attention, ready to run from behind the car, when a new sound checked his progress. The deep, heavy roar of a diesel engine.

The Spaniard must have heard it too, as he started to swing the gun away from Spike. But he was too slow: emerging from the fog was the bonnet of a black van, headlamps on, moving at speed. The van veered off the road, wheels kicking up shingle before its bumper collided with the Spaniard's waist. There was a nauseating crunch, and Spike watched as the Spaniard flew backwards, arms held gracefully aloft as he looped through the air, like a child playing at aeroplanes.

Spike ducked back behind the boot as he felt the Spaniard thump down next to him, rolling then coming to a final halt against the low cliff wall. The headlights of the van shone onto his face as he lay on the shingle, head turned towards Spike. His glasses were gone now, and Spike could see that he was probably in his early thirties, his handsome face marred only by a disdainful curl of the upper lip. With his dyed grey hair and cheap clothes, Spike might have passed him in town a hundred times, or never. The man gazed back, perplexed, frown lines still creasing his tanned brow. He tried to raise his head, but a gush of dark blood was starting to ooze from the back of his skull, his face covered in a clammy sheen. '*Puta*,' Spike saw him mouth before he closed his eyes.

On the road above, Spike heard the van door slam. He kept his head down behind the SEAT, trying not to look at the Spaniard's body, the wiry arms twisted at a grotesque angle, gloved hands open and empty. Where was the pistol?

Footsteps crunched across the shingle. Spike fumbled on the ground around the car, desperately feeling for the gun. The footsteps stopped, and Spike heard a scraping as the van driver crouched to pick something up. Then a metallic click as the barrel of the pistol was expertly checked, and the walking resumed. Spike lay still and held his breath.

A stiff, familiar figure loomed above the body of the Spaniard. 'Fucking hell fire,' Jardine murmured as he stared down at the stranger he had just run over. A faint knocking came from above Spike's head, and Jardine swung round and trained the gun on the boot of the SEAT. It was then that Spike decided to run.

Chapter Fifty-two

Jardine was thrown off balance as Spike sprinted out from behind the car. He felt the shingle turn to tarmac beneath his feet, and knew he had made it up onto the road. Breaking the fog to his left was the mangled netting of the cricket pitch; Spike headed towards it as a first shot rang out, the bullet fizzing off the road just a few yards in front of him. His joints and muscles responded automatically, and he veered the opposite way.

Another gunshot, an impact to Spike's right, so he changed direction again, sensing the beam of the lighthouse sweep over the back of his head, revealing the Rock in front, rolling with mist, massive and powerful, beckoning with a promise of safety.

The van door slammed, and Spike pulled off the road, running uphill through the Rock scrub, nostrils filling with the reassuring scent of pine resin and musty ape spoor. An engine revved, and he slipped in fear, gashing his knee on a ridge of limestone. Another gunshot thudded into the loose soil above Spike's head. He lurched sideways, vaguely aware – despite his panic – that either Captain Jardine must be a terrible shot or was deliberately steering him towards a particular location.

The van was trailing him now along the coast road, perhaps looking for a clearer line of fire. The Rock began to grow steeper, and Spike crouched by an outcrop, pausing for breath. The lighthouse rotated again. He glanced up and saw the track that led up to the tunnel mouth. The grille was open.

Another shot; Spike waited for the burning pain that would bring an end to it all, grateful at least that Jardine was focusing on him rather than the small boy still locked in the boot of the SEAT. Then he realised that no one else knew Charlie was there, and he increased his pace, moving crabwise through the scrub, pushing apart the claws of an agave until he found himself standing on the loose flattened earth of the track.

Another blast, this one so close that it blew dust onto Spike's bloody knee. He clambered upwards to the tunnel mouth, climbed inside then grabbed hold of the hinged bars and pulled them towards him. Below, the headlights of the van dazzled his eyes as it fought its way up the slope. The grille closed and Spike reached for the clasp. The padlock was gone.

The van was just ten yards away. Spike glanced back into the tunnel, seeing a broad concrete roadway, wide enough for a lorry. He realised now why the grille was open. The van must have driven out of it: that was how it had appeared so mysteriously beside the viewing platform. Judging by the speed with which it was now approaching, the driver was planning a return visit. Spinning on his heel, Spike started to run down the tunnel, plunging deep into the belly of the Rock.

Chapter Fifty-three

A distant glow came from the end of the tunnel. Spike ran towards it, feeling tepid water from the roof dripping onto his head, soaking his hair – last year's rainfall finally working its way through the limestone. The tunnel was broad and straight, heading westwards, Spike calculated; it ought to come out by Little Bay, though whether the grille would be open on the other side was a different question. He heard the rumble of the van behind him and peered back, seeing two bright beams of yellow piercing the darkness. The engine roared, deliberately over-revved. Then the van began accelerating down the tunnel towards him.

Spike stumbled on, feet splashing on the damp floor, glancing left and right at the sidewalls as the light from the van began to leach along them. The limestone had been concreted over, a rusty handrail running up one side. Could Spike dive under it? Out of the van's path? Not enough room. The engine revved again, and Spike increased his speed, seeing a crisscross shape twenty yards ahead. Another grille, blocking the tunnel midway down.

He shook the bars, lungs burning, gulping for air. This time the padlock was in place. He looked around: the van was still coming, slower now, as though the driver had realised that less force was needed to crush a man than to run him down. But in the light of the headlamps, Spike saw a smaller tunnel branching to the left, beginning at chest height, disappearing into darkness.

Moments before the van was upon him, Spike dived into the side tunnel and drove himself onwards. The blackness was total, then a single yellow beam began to emerge from behind. The light flickered: a handheld torch.

'Keep going, Gibbo,' came Jardine's amused voice.

Spike could only obey, crawling now. The floor grew softer, moist and clay-like. It started to widen out, so he rose to his feet, hand flailing to the sidewall, recoiling sharply as what looked like a butcher's hook pierced his palm. A line of S-shaped prongs ran up the walls – cable-holders for cables that were no longer there.

He almost missed the opening to his right: a broader tunnel with caged strip lights on the roof, extending like cats' eyes on an inverted motorway. There were more roads inside the Rock than out, he remembered – thirty-three miles in total. A few of the ceiling lights were on, so he veered inside, relieved finally to be able to see where he was going.

The temperature fell as the tunnel sank deeper inside the Rock. Spike glanced back, dreading the sound that would mean Jardine was gaining. But he heard no footsteps, saw not a flicker of a torch. Suddenly he made out a new noise, not from behind, but from in front, a low ghostly wail. The tunnels were said to be haunted: even the apes would not go in – if a baby monkey strayed inside its parents would remain at the mouth, frantically chattering, unable to follow. A group of estate kids had snuck through an open grille off Castle Road last year. But the cries they'd heard had turned out to be British soldiers, covertly training in cave warfare before being deployed to Afghanistan. It was a miracle the children hadn't been shot, the papers said.

The wailing persisted, louder now, and Spike forced himself to move forwards, T-shirt clinging to his chest, soaked with stinking water and sweat. The amorphous sound began to form itself into voices, and now he could tell where they were coming from: to his right, a newer-looking gate gave off the tunnel into a large, well-lit chamber. Spike crouched beside it, staring through the bars in amazement. Inside, on the concrete floor, lay tens of grey plastic tubs; beyond, by an old army Nissen hut, two white vans were parked, rear doors open, 'Europcar' marked in green on each side. The Stay Behind Cave, Spike realised. From the back of one of the vans stepped a tall lean man in wipe-clean clothing.

'Get a move on,' Clohessy barked, and Dougie the Scot appeared at once from the Nissen hut, three heavy crates stacked in his arms. So Neptune were getting the salvage out of Gib early. But how? Spike remembered talk of a private plane. Yet all aircraft were grounded due to Charlie's disappearance. By land? The border with Spain was closed.

'You there, Gibbo?' echoed a call from behind. Spike had time to see Clohessy swivel at the sound of Jardine's voice before he sprinted away past the gate.

The tunnel started to climb upwards inside the Rock. The roof lights suddenly went out. Spike fumbled for a handrail, then pressed on in the dark.

A few yards on, a dull glow threw a little light on the tunnel floor, revealing a smaller shaft angling upwards, the air inside cleaner-smelling, pinpricks of what looked like starlight at its end. Spike hauled himself inside. If this was a ventilation shaft, as he suspected, then it would emerge on the side of the Rock, hopefully with no grille to block it.

Tiring now, Spike started to drag himself along the passageway, feeling the uneven surface of the stone beneath his palms, a sign that the shaft had been bored by hand, part of the original eighteenth-century network built to defend the Rock during the Great Siege.

The roof lowered, forcing him to crawl again, his injured knee dragging blood along the floor, his steady rhythmic progress allowing his mind to wander, first back to Tangiers, when he'd rescued Zahra from the path of the jeep, then to Malta, where an ancient escape route beneath a knight's palazzo had saved him from a fire. A warm, salty breeze started to blow onto his face, and at last he was able to draw in the sweet air of Gibraltar, of home. The tunnel broadened again, and now he could see the moon above, hear the distant sounds of the city, the murmur of waves at the foot of the Rock.

Spike raised himself into a standing position and stepped towards the open tunnel mouth. One hand gripping an iron rung, he peered down, seeing a sheer drop, the razor wire of the military base below.

There was less fog on this side of the Rock. As Spike looked out further, he made out a thin escarpment to the left, leading down the eastern face of the moutain. If he could somehow swing down to it, he had a chance.

Pulling off his sodden T-shirt, he started to roll it up, preparing to tie it to the rung. Then he heard a triumphant voice behind him: 'Gotcha.'

Chapter Fifty-four

Captain Hugh Jardine stood at the entrance to the cavern. He wore old grey sweatpants and black trainers. Wrapped around his waist was a fleece, perhaps removed as the chase had progressed. Clenched in his hand was a pistol, pointing at Spike's naked chest.

Spike took a backwards step, feeling the breeze from the open tunnel chill the sweat on his shoulders.

'Sorry about your friend in the SEAT,' Jardine panted. 'I thought he was you. Or perhaps that was what you intended?' Jardine glanced down at the mother-of-pearl handle of the gun. 'He had good taste in firearms, whoever he was.'

'The police will find the body.'

'You think so? I dumped it over the seawall. And they didn't spend much time investigating the last hit-and-run, did they?' Jardine must have seen something in Spike's expression as he slimmed his eyes and chuckled. 'I thought you'd worked that out. Turned out your business partner was the only lawyer in history who couldn't be bought off.'

Spike risked a glance at the open drop behind. 'Did you bring Simon Grainger up here?'

'Now there was a man who knew the value of money,' Jardine said. 'He came to see me and Mort. Got wind that we'd found some silver and said he knew it was Spanish. We didn't take him seriously at first, but then we found out about his other discoveries. The ship's bell. Some pieces of eight.'

The pistol was now pointing at Spike's throat. Why hadn't Jardine fired it? No one would hear the shot.

'So you killed him.'

'We did consider paying him off. Brought him up here to see the coins before we melted them down. Then he told us he'd met with your friend, Galliano.' He sighed. 'And that was that.'

'So you jacked him up on Zoloft and alcohol and threw him over the edge.'

Jardine laughed. 'We got him drunk all right. But he took the happy pills on his own time.' He shrugged. 'Call it a lucky break.'

Spike thought back to the wedding photograph in the Graingers' apartment. The gentle giant gazing tenderly into his young wife's face, Amy's veil thrown back as she met his eyes. Both dead now, murdered so that rich men could keep their dirty secrets hidden. Spike made no effort to temper the contempt in his voice. 'So who came up with the scheme to steal the silver?'

'That was Mort's idea. I just helped with logistics.' Jardine raised an eyebrow. 'The execution, if you like.' He was enjoying himself now. 'Mort told me they'd found Spanish treasure near the *Gloucester* wreck. He wanted to find a way for Neptune to claim it. Turned out to be a little more complicated than we hoped. But here we are. Stop doing that, will you?'

Spike was edging away from the tunnel mouth, eyes roving for a loose cable hook.

'And keep your hands up. Palms open.'

Spike stepped back in front of the opening, hearing the breeze howl through the crags below.

'There'll be no trouble attributing *your* death to suicide,' Jardine went on. 'Like mother, like son.' He took a step closer. 'She would have fucked me eventually, you know. They all did, back then. But she was a drunk. Completely crackers, as it turned out. But then you know all that, don't you?' He cocked the gun and said softly, 'It's close to here, isn't it, where her car went over the cliff? There's an appealing symmetry in that at least.'

Spike felt his heel pivot on the tunnel edge. 'I still have the ship's bell,' he said quickly, playing for time.

Jardine paused, considering.

'You wanted it enough to kill Grainger.'

'Grainger was a two-bit blackmailer.'

'And to have Dougie break into my house. I've got it with me here. I'm sure Mort would be pleased to see it destroyed.'

'Where?'

'There. Just behind me.'

In the fraction of a second that Jardine's eyes flicked to the left, Spike threw his weight forward against the old soldier's arm. They both watched in silence as the pistol arced through the air. Then Spike launched himself at Jardine's stomach.

They fell together on the cool stone floor, Jardine immediately rolling over, his muscles unexpectedly taut. He stretched out a hand for the pistol, but Spike held him back, trying to pull him away, face pressed into his fleece, catching the lonely smell of smoke and booze trapped within. Jardine's fingers were edging forwards, just an inch from the gun now; Spike released him for a moment, then dug the nails of both hands deep into the scar he'd been shown on the pontoon. Jardine let out a desperate groan, arms clutching his side; as soon as he loosened his grip on the floor, Spike hauled him round, surprised at the lightness of the man, and shoved him forward until his head was sticking out over the edge of the open tunnel mouth.

'Please,' Jardine called back, words muffled by the breeze, 'I'll pay you.' Now his chest was dangling out from the Rock. 'I'll give you everything Mort paid me. Four hundred thousand pounds.'

Spike held onto Jardine's legs as his upper body sank further into the void.

'It's in a Cayman Islands account,' he called out in a high-pitched voice. 'We can make a deal . . .'

Spike felt Jardine's legs lurch forward. His black trainers caught in the crooks of Spike's arms. His weight was dragging Spike towards the edge; he held on for a moment, then released his grip, seeing Jardine's feet vanish almost instantly into the darkness. There was a distant cry, followed by a soft, hollow thump.

Spike sat back. The pistol was beside him. He kicked it out after Jardine, then waited for his breathing to steady.

Chapter Fifty-five

Gripping the material of his rolled-up T-shirt, Spike swung through the night air. At the last moment, he released his make-shift rope and landed awkwardly on the thin strip of land to the left of the tunnel mouth, bare chest catching against the trunk of a holm-oak tree. Tentatively he got to his feet and started the slow painful climb down the eastern flank of the Rock.

With the moon shining down, and the breeze warm against his bleeding skin, Spike felt as though he were in a dream. His senses were heightened, his mind sharp, the objects around him hyperreal. He considered this ancient Rock where he'd been born, stuck between continents and oceans, between cultures and races, with its jungle of monkeys and lawyers and children and soldiers and crooks and tourists. The Rock was like the earth, he thought, spinning in infinity with no one the wiser as to why it existed, how it made sense, what these strange and arbitrary collisions meant. For a moment he felt as though he was at the centre of the universe, bound up with it. Then he pushed through the fronds of a fan palm and saw Hugh Jardine's shattered body on the ground.

The dead man lay in the foetal position, a spill of blood and other matter seeping into the pebbly scrub beneath him. His right wrist was folded back where he had put out his hands to try to break his fall, and his left ... Spike raised his head and saw the silhouette of an ape sitting on a crag, a tubular object gripped between its paws.

Forcing his eyes away, he knelt at the remains of Jardine's corpse. A raw, butcher's shop stink rose from his chest. Keeping his eyes averted from the stump, Spike pulled off the fleece wrapped around Jardine's waist and slipped it over his own shoulders, then brushed a hand over the man's pockets. Car keys, wallet, smartphone in a rubber case. The device appeared miraculously unscathed. Spike tapped in a number, wondering at the clarity of his mind, the ease with which he remembered each digit.

'DS Navarro?' came a voice at the end of the line.

'It's me.'

'Spike? Where are you?'

'It doesn't matter. I've found Charlie.'

'*What*?'

'He's locked in the boot of a blue SEAT parked on the viewing platform at Europa Point. He's alive, Jess.'

'Jesus.' He could hear the relief flooding into her voice. 'Just wait a minute, will you? Just wait.'

Spike stared out from the Rock as he listened to Jessica shouting commands to her colleagues. To his right, he saw Black Strap Cove, Both Worlds retirement village alongside. He shook his head in amazement: he must have passed through the entire breadth of the Rock. A ship was moored off the jetty by Sandy Bay – hulking industrial hull, black gantry crane rising from the stern . . .

'There's an ambulance on the way,' Jessica said.

'Make sure they bring fluids.'

'I will.'

A smaller vessel was approaching the jetty, and Spike recognised the RIB that had taken him out to the *Trident* on the day he had first met Mort Clohessy. 'Are you still on boat patrol?' he asked.

'Just back.'

'Can you turn round and pick me up on the jetty in Sandy Bay?'

'Why would I want to do that, Spike? I've been up for the last twenty-four hours.'

'Because I'm about to hand you the biggest bust of your career.'

Chapter Fifty-six

Spike paced the jetty as he watched the Royal Gibraltar Police launch crash towards him over the waves. In the distance he could just make out the tail lights of the *Trident* as she sailed away through Gibraltar territorial seas.

The police launch slowed by the jetty, Jessica standing in the back, Inspector George Isola at the wheel.

'Get in,' Jessica called, and Spike climbed into the boat, grimacing as he pulled his injured knee over the fibreglass rim. The strange epiphany he had experienced on the Rock had now been eclipsed by a dull persistent headache throbbing against the top of his skull. 'Did you find him?' he shouted. 'Did you find the boy?'

Jessica nodded, and Spike tried to interpret her expression. 'For fuck's sake, Jess. Tell me! Is Charlie all right?'

She nodded again, and Spike enjoyed a brief moment of relief before he felt his arms yanked behind his back and the cold steel of handcuffs pinch his wrists. 'You're under arrest,' Isola said, perhaps more enthusiastically than might have been considered professional.

'What's the charge, George?' Spike said, looking at Jessica, eyebrows raised.

'Withholding information. Suspicion of kidnap . . .'

'Tell me he's joking, Jess.'

Jessica averted her eyes as Isola shoved Spike down onto the rear seat of the boat. Turning away, Spike nodded towards the lights of the *Trident* fading into the distance. 'Oi! Genius! You need to intercept that ship,' he shouted at Isola. 'The real baddies are getting away.'

But Isola ignored him and fired up the engine, a smile of satisfaction on his face.

'What are you *talking* about?' Jessica said.

'That ship is carrying illegally raised bullion. Melted-down pieces of eight.'

Isola glanced around and rolled his eyes.

'There's also ivory aboard,' Spike said. 'In breach of the Convention on International Trade in Endangered Species.'

Isola slipped the launch into gear and began steering it along the coastline towards Gibraltar Harbour.

'There's a body, you *cortapisha*,' Spike shouted. 'Under the cliffs by Europa Point Lighthouse. It belongs to the man who took Charlie. The men aboard the *Trident* killed him.' He turned to Jessica. 'For fuck's sake, Jess! Can you do something?'

Jessica stared back, then made her way over to Isola. At first he threw up his arms like an angry teenager, but then she placed a hand on his shoulder and, like many a man before him, he weakened. Throwing Spike a look, he put the boat into neutral and took out his radio. A moment later, he was standing by Spike's side. No taller than five-foot-seven, Spike was pleased to note.

'You're talking about the cargo ship that just passed us, right?' Isola said, pointing at a flashing red light disappearing into the darkness.

'About fifteen minutes ago, yes.'

Isola barked into his radio, then clambered back to the wheel. Jessica sat down by Spike as the police launch picked up speed, slamming over the waves. 'Is that blood?' she said, pointing at the creeping stain on the knee of his cargo trousers.

He nodded, eyes trained on the ship's lights. They were catching her up now; Spike arched his head and checked their position. The port of Algeciras glittered to the right – the *Trident* was pressing into the open Mediterranean as it sought to leave Gibraltar seas.

'You can still make an arrest in international waters,' Spike called to the front of the boat. 'Universal jurisdiction.'

Isola nodded impatiently, then swore as he watched the *Trident* change direction. Spike thought back to the map he'd studied for the Neptune case delineating Gibraltar territorial seas. There was a thin buffer zone of international waters between Gibraltarian and Spanish territory, but the space beyond that belonged categorically to Spain. Isola must have known it too, as he jammed the engine into full throttle and flicked on the police light on the roof. Soon the *Trident* would be in Spanish territory, an impossible location for the Gibraltar police to make an arrest in without triggering an international incident.

Fettered by his handcuffs, Spike slid from side to side, leg aching with each jolt, the wind chilling his neck. Jessica put out a hand to steady him, her touch warm and comforting. Half a mile ahead, the *Trident* had completed its arc. Spike made out the gallows shape of the gantry crane and saw the RIB bouncing behind it, dragged by a rope from the stern.

Isola slowed, frowning at a computerised map on the control panel. '*Bezims*,' he cursed, smashing the tiller with a fist.

'Spanish waters,' Jessica said to Spike.

Spike thought for a moment, then smiled. 'But the ship's carrying Spanish silver.'

Jessica stared back, baffled.

'Radio the Guardia Civil,' Spike called to the front of the launch, feeling a wave of fatigue hit him at the prospect of having to explain a complex point of international maritime law to Inspector Isola. 'Tell them that a boat carrying stolen Spanish artefacts has just entered Spanish territorial waters. Come on!'

Jessica hesitated, then took out her radio. A moment later she spoke in her near-perfect Spanish, watched by her mute and puzzled superior. Spike glanced again towards land. They were two miles from Algeciras now; with the *Trident* heading west, soon she'd be out of Spanish waters altogether and onto the

Moroccan side of the Straits, beyond the jurisdiction even of the Guardia Civil.

'The ship's called the *Trident*, right?' Jessica called to Spike. He nodded, and she spoke more urgently into her radio. Before she'd even hung up, Spike caught a high-pitched rattle in the distance, like ball bearings shaken in a jar. A small flashing light started bombing towards them out of the bay. They sat in silence and watched as the noise grew louder. A minute later, a powerful Guardia Civil patrol boat roared by, the silhouette of a machine-gun mount rising on its rear deck.

'They've got the gunboat out,' Isola called back with unembarrassed excitement, putting his own engine into gear and following the Guardia at a respectful distance.

The echo of a loudhailer reverberated across the water, but the *Trident* pressed on, ignoring whatever Spanish threats were being issued at volume.

'Refusal to stop,' Isola called back. 'They can arrest them for that alone.'

The loudhailer sounded again, followed by a crackle of gunfire, rubber bullets shot into the air as a warning. In the distance, the lights of the Moroccan shoreline grew stronger – the port city of Tetouan, drawing closer. Spike watched the Guardia boat speed around the bow of the *Trident*, blocking her route, blue and red lights flashing. But rather than relent, the *Trident* continued bearing down on it.

Spike imagined the testosterone of the control room, Clohessy screaming, Dougie mumbling Scottish curses as little Jamie covered his eyes and prayed for his mother. At the last moment, the Guardia boat seemed to lose its nerve and revved away. There was an unsettling silence as the *Trident* chugged on, unencumbered, but then a moment later they heard a deeper burst of gunfire, then a series of ominous thumps.

The Guardia boat stopped, swaying in the current as the *Trident* powered onwards, its shape fading into the gloom. 'They must be in Moroccan waters now,' Isola said. 'Game over.'

A sudden fizzing sound cut through the sky as a phosphorescent glow appeared above. Spike, Jessica and Isola got to their feet, watching as the distress flare hung motionless, then exploded into crimson light. And then Spike realised that the bow of the *Trident* was strangely high in the water, her gantry crane pitching forward, tipping her upwards. On either side of the ship, he saw figures floundering in the reddened water, then the flare died and the figures were hidden again by a terrible darkness.

Jessica spoke into her radio and called to Isola. He nodded, then gunned the engine and began speeding towards the stricken ship.

Chapter Fifty-seven

Mayday was evidently an international signal – derived from the French, 'M'aidez', Spike seemed to remember as he stared out from the Royal Gibraltar Police launch, feeling his wrists chafe as the salt water sprayed onto his tight handcuffs. As they neared the *Trident*, he made out a rusty Italian container ship floating alongside the Guardia gunboat. On the opposite coastline, a Moroccan patrol vessel was powering towards them from Tetouan, along with a helicopter that must have come from Ceuta, one of two Spanish enclaves in Morocco, the existence of which – in Gibraltarian eyes – rendered all Spanish complaints about the Rock null and void.

The gantry crane appeared to have pulled the RIB under as well, as what looked like the entire crew of the *Trident* had now abandoned ship. The Spanish lifeguards were already hauling men from the water; Spike saw their spotlight flash onto a blue polo shirt and recognised the shaggy blond form of Anders the Swede being pulled into the back of the boat.

A smaller group of survivors seemed to have become separated from the rest. The Italian container ship's lifeboat was rowing towards them, two sturdy men in oilskins manning the oars. Isola reduced the throttle and steered the police launch their way.

As they passed what was left of the *Trident*, a last creak came from her bow as she slipped completely under the water. Waves bulged, jolting Spike and Jessica in the back of the launch. For a moment Spike lost sight of the men in the water, then saw heads re-emerge as the surface settled. Isola twisted the engine in bursts, fearful of running over any survivors.

By the time they'd drawn up by the Italian lifeboat, there was only one man left in the water. One of the Italians was reaching down to him; Spike saw a pale face bob up, breaking the surface like an egg. Jamie was on his feet in the lifeboat, thin hair drenched as he screamed at the man in the water, 'Take it off, for God's sake! Take it off!'

Isola steered the police launch closer. Overhead, the Spanish helicopter arrived, searchlight illuminating the scene as a rope ladder was lowered into the water.

'Take off the rucksack!' Jamie cried.

The Italian lost the man's grip, and he disappeared again below the surface. His colleague was stripping down now, yelling instructions as the Guardia Civil boat pulled up, all other members of the Neptune crew rescued and remaindered below deck.

Spike peered over the edge of the launch and saw a man's thin white face bob up in the water. He recognised the strong jaw and stubborn brow of Morton D. Clohessy. Clohessy's mouth broke the surface, sucking in air like a carp, brown island of hair furrowed as he fought to stay afloat. Looped over his chest, Spike made out the straps of a rucksack, so tight against his shoulders that it had to contain something dense and heavy – metal perhaps. He wondered if Clohessy had seen him as he seemed to open his mouth to speak. But a moment later, a wave from the Guardia speedboat rolled over him, and he sank back down, face fading as he disappeared into the depths of the water.

'Why didn't you help him, for Chrissake?' Isola yelled.

Turning his back on Isola, Spike stretched out his cuffed hands behind him. The Italian swam towards their boat, performing an impressive breaststroke. '*Dov'è?*' he called up. '*Dov'è!*'

Isola cursed, scouring the water, as a frogman started abseiling down the helicopter's rope ladder. A tannoy from the cockpit ordered all boats to move away, first in Spanish, then in Moroccan,

Italian, and lastly, reluctantly, in English. Isola turned the police launch round, withdrawing in the direction of Gibraltar.

Spike remained at the stern, staring at the helicopter as it hovered over the location where Clohessy and his ship had sunk. Jessica sat down beside him. 'We've just had confirmation. They've found another body. Up on the Rock.'

Spike nodded.

Jessica stared at him. 'How did you know?'

'Know what?'

'Where to find the boy.' Her dark eyes questioned his, then she pulled a small bunch of keys out of her pocket and undid his handcuffs. 'Charlie's in hospital,' she said, tucking the cuffs into her belt. 'For observation. Under police guard.'

'Will you take me to see him?'

She took his right hand, caressing the bruise on the back and the raw skin around his wrist. Then her fingers interlinked with his, enfolding his palm and giving it a gentle squeeze. After a moment's hesitation, Spike returned the pressure. The lights on the Rock seemed to brighten as they headed for home.

*

I hear water lap against stones, feel it whipping up from time to time into a foamy spray as unseen ships pass in the distance. The beam of the lighthouse, still turning, picks out the dark surface of the sea. I cannot move. My face is wet. When I stick out my tongue, I taste not saltwater, but a ferrous tang I have come to know well.

How many did I kill, I wonder now. Twenty? Perhaps one more, if they do not find the boy. It has occurred to me sometimes, usually in the night, that they might have suffered, felt pain or fear. But now as I lie here, I realise that I have nothing with which to reproach myself. The coming of death is peaceful. We are no different to the pebbles beneath my head – we wash up, we grind down, the world rolls on. If there is a scheme, perhaps I have contributed to it no less than most. Who can say? Millennia will pass before that sort of thing is clear.

I hear a noise from the cliffs above. The lighthouse rotates again, and I try to raise my head, then feel a sticky warmth run from my scalp, filling the cavities of my ears. Voices now – English, of course. A sudden pain starts to climb from my legs to my chest, and I let out a sigh. The irony of it . . . For it to end here, of all places. I, Rodrigo de Guzmán, direct descendant of the great conquistador, one-time captain of the Spanish police, killer of twenty, perhaps twenty-one, am to die on the shores of a stolen British colony. And suddenly I see how Gibraltar can still exist. The effrontery of it, the cheek – that can only be pulled off by a strange and resilient race. It is my fault. I should have taken more care.

I try to think of Madrid, of the Prado with the sun setting over the Plaza Mayor. But no. I will die here. In Gibraltar. Then – silence.

Chapter Fifty-eight

Spike sat in a windowless interview room at the back of New Mole House, watching Inspector George Isola struggle to adjust the sound level on his tape recorder. 'Tell me again about the ship,' Isola resumed.

'The *Trident*,' Spike said. 'Owned by a company called Neptune Marine. They were using her to salvage lead from a wreck sunk in the Straits. What the company failed to disclose was that they had also been plundering Spanish silver from an adjacent shipwreck.'

'And you were helping them do this?'

Spike took a steadying breath, feeling the cuts on his chest test the steri-strips the nurse had applied the night before. 'I represented Neptune Marine in relation to their legitimate salvage of the *Gloucester*. What I discovered only later was that the crew were melting down the Spanish coins in an attempt to pass them off as part of the same cargo.'

'I see,' Isola replied uncertainly, jotting something down in his notebook. He looked like he'd had a much better night's sleep than Spike. 'And how is the boy connected?' he asked.

'His father was Simon Grainger – remember him?'

'Of course,' Isola retorted.

'Grainger realised what Neptune were up to. Tried to get in on the action. So Jardine lured him into the Rock and killed him. Made it look like suicide. He had similar plans for me.'

'But in fact it was you who killed Jardine.'

'In self-defence.'

More assiduous note-taking; Spike found himself wondering what Isola thought the tape recorder was for.

'And your belief is that Jardine must have killed Mrs Grainger too. And kidnapped her son. Why would he do that?'

The lie came at once to Spike's lips. 'In order to keep me quiet. Jardine knew that I was involved with Amy Grainger, and that I'd learnt about Neptune's crimes. The Graingers provided the perfect collateral to buy my silence.'

'Why not just kill you?'

Spike was momentarily taken aback by the acuity of Isola's question. 'He tried to, didn't he? On the Rock. His prints were on the pistol.'

Isola paused, then slowly nodded. 'And the body found on Deadman's Beach?'

'I have no idea. Possibly an accomplice of Jardine's.'

'Why kill him if he was an accomplice?'

'He knew too much. As did Simon Grainger. As did I.'

'And your business partner?'

'Exactly,' Spike said. 'Peter was Neptune's original lawyer. Grainger went to see him – told him what he'd found out. When Jardine learnt about it, he got Peter drunk, then ran him over and passed it off as a random hit-and-run.'

Isola fixed Spike with a stare, and he looked away, scanning the rows of posters and mugshots hanging on the wall, evidence of the hard work of the Royal Gibraltar Police – drugs intercepted from Morocco, cigarette smugglers arrested, domestic abusers locked up. Why not just tell him that the dead Spaniard had been hired by Žigon? he wondered. Then he looked back and watched Isola pick a piece of breakfast from between his teeth. Better to let Interpol handle it.

'How were Neptune Marine paying Jardine?' Isola asked, tongue still roving around his mouth.

'I have no idea, Inspector. I should have thought that was your job. While we were up on the Rock, Jardine did mention an account in the Cayman Islands. I expect that you'll find that the payer was Clohessy.'

'The drowned man.'

'Before he drowned.'

Spike watched Isola try to think of something with which to admonish him, then abandon the search.

'Do I need to instruct a lawyer, Inspector Isola? Because unless you're planning to charge me with something, I think I've spent enough time voluntarily helping the police with their enquiries.'

Isola clicked off the tape recorder and got to his feet. 'I've always had a good bullshit detector,' he said quietly. 'And it's going off right now.'

'Neptune were running a complicated operation,' Spike replied. 'I realise it must be difficult for you to keep up.'

As Spike pulled open the door, he felt Isola's glare intensify as he saw Jessica get up from a plastic chair in the waiting room, and accompany him into another sunlit Gibraltar morning.

PART THREE

Genoa

Chapter Fifty-nine

Spike Sanguinetti stared out of the window, identifying the Balearic Islands below, Minorca at the head of the chain, ceded to Britain three centuries ago under the same treaty as Gibraltar, now returned to Spanish rule. Just another chess piece of the Mediterranean, shifted by naval superpowers jostling for prominence. How many lives had been changed by these baffling political moves, families uprooted, strange races formed?

'Sir?' The smiling stewardess was back at his elbow. It was a busy flight yet she seemed remarkably solicitous of Spike's needs. 'Another tomato juice?'

'Thanks.'

'Want any vodka in this one?'

Spike shook his head as the ice-filled plastic cup appeared. What was it about planes and tomato juice? He never had any desire to drink the stuff on land, yet up in the sky he couldn't get enough of it. He reached for his briefcase and pulled out the documents he'd received from his contact at Interpol. In some ways, the situation had worked out better than he could have hoped. The scanned image of Žigon he had sent to Interpol had tallied with the driver's licence of a man pulled over for racing his Lamborghini Aventador in Genoa. Once an identification had been made, armed police had arrived at Žigon's opulent townhouse on the Via Garibaldi to question him over the death of a hotel doorman, whose decomposing body had been found face-down in the Gulf of Genoa. A firefight had ensued in which

Žigon – now believed to be a former member of Slovenian special forces – had been gravely wounded, and three of his henchmen killed. Žigon was currently in intensive care at an undisclosed hospital, awaiting trial. Spike stared down at the blurred photocopy of Žigon's driving licence. His real name was Aleksander Zavrl.

The greater challenge for the Italian police had been trying to unravel Žigon's financial dealings. It was clear that he'd been trying to reinvent himself as a legitimate businessman, siphoning the fortune he had stockpiled from drug and prostitution rackets into an offshore company in Monaco, which was greedily snapping up commercial property all along the Italian Riviera. Most of this had already been seized by an impecunious Italian government. The question now was what other assets they could link to him.

No trace of a Zahra al-Mahmoud had been found in Žigon's townhouse, nor was her name known to any of his contacts. As a last resort, Spike had asked his friend at Interpol if there were any residential properties contained in Žigon's portfolio. Two apartment blocks, it emerged, one in Genoa, one in San Remo, plus a smattering of villas along the Italian coastline. None of the tenants had matched Zahra's description; all would shortly face eviction, with the Italian government selling its spoils to the highest bidder. One address had caught Spike's eye, however. A house in a village called Ruta. Though Spike hadn't heard of the place, he'd since found out that the nearest town was Portofino.

The sound of the name brought a hot sting of sweat to Spike's forehead. He reached up to adjust the nozzle of the ceiling fan. *Žigon would never hurt me*, Zahra had once said. What had previously been a source of pain was now the only thing Spike could cling to.

The stewardess reappeared. Her platinum hair was twisted viciously into a knot, and Spike found himself wondering again why anyone would choose to conceal such a delicate prettiness under an indelible layer of orange pancake and waterproof mascara.

'Can I tempt you to any duty-free?' she said.

'No thanks; I'm from Gibraltar,' Spike offered by way of explanation.

The stewardess pushed her lip-glossed mouth into a smile. 'We were trying to guess where you were from. Haven't you got your own airport?'

'It only flies to the UK. Hence the departure from Málaga.'

The stewardess draped a bare arm over the top of Spike's seat. 'And what are you up to in Genoa?'

'Unfinished business.'

'Sounds intriguing.' She must have caught his glance at the trolley: 'Sure you don't want a proper drink?'

'No. Thank you. Really.' He forced a polite smile, then turned back to the window, seeing the brown landmass of Corsica below, first Genoese, then British, now French. He realised that he hadn't smoked a cigarette, nor had a drink, since the night the *Trident* sank four weeks ago. He hadn't missed it much, and it had helped him to analyse what had happened with a clearer eye.

Certain things had worked out well. Peter's recovery was proceeding steadily. The doctors said he would always walk with a cane, and would have to undergo many months of intensive rehabilitation, including relearning to drive, which Spike might have suggested even before the accident. Most importantly, his mental faculties appeared unscathed. He had managed to keep off the weight, and there was even talk of him returning to work early next year. In Peter's absence, Spike had thrown himself into a series of banal conveyancing and tax cases, and the revenues of Galliano & Sanguinetti were now back in the black. They could pay the rent, at least.

Rufus was also improving. Ever since he had told Spike about his sister, Juliet, he'd seemed more at peace with himself. Now the two of them could sit quietly together in a room, his father painting again, Spike working, even reading the occasional novel, something he hadn't done in years. Next month, on the anniversary of Spike's mother's death, they were planning to visit both graves at the cemetery.

As for Charlie Grainger, there was good news there too, if you looked hard enough. It turned out that the *Trident* had sunk just inside Spanish waters, and the local *junta* had put in an immediate claim for salvage. With the support of Counsel for the Crown, Drew Stanford-Trench, Spike had cooperated with the Spanish authorities, and the copper content of the silver bars raised from the seabed had been matched to that of the *peso de ocho* from the *Flos Sanctus Montis*, the identity of which was confirmed by the ship's bell. Spike had instructed a reputable firm of Spanish solicitors to have Simon Grainger recognised as the original finder of the wreck. As both Simon and his wife were dead, the sole heir would be Charlie Grainger.

Spike had visited the boy a few times at his grandparents' house on Horse Barrack Lane. He remained guarded and silent, but for some reason he seemed to like Spike, and was content to sit on his knee reading or colouring. On his last visit, Spike had mentioned the claim, explaining that Charlie could be due a payout of between 5 and 10 per cent of the value of the silver. The grandparents had looked stupefied as Spike had floated a potential award of two million euros, after tax. The possibility of a trust fund had been mooted, with Spike appointed as trustee. Whatever happened, he would ensure that the boy was looked after.

As for Neptune Marine . . . Its stock price had plummeted as news broke internationally, and a vulture fund had seized control. Within days, the company had been rebranded and all its previous sins laid firmly at the door of the late CEO, Morton D. Clohessy. The argument for this was compelling: Clohessy had been so desperate to land a big score to put Neptune back on an even financial keel that he'd lost all sense of proportion, committing crime after crime to keep his business afloat. He'd found a like-minded accomplice in Captain Hugh Jardine. A journeyman soldier, Jardine had been incensed to find so many of his former colleagues earning huge sums of money working for private defence contractors, while he was stuck in a desk job in Gibraltar, in constant pain from an injury suffered during the Falklands War. Following his interview with Spike, Inspector George Isola of the Royal Gibraltar Police had unearthed a series of large illegal payments made to Jardine by Clohessy in a Cayman Islands account. Isola had also been congratulated for matching a paint sample from the scene of Peter Galliano's accident to a scratch on the chassis of Jardine's van.

The enduring mystery surrounded the body found below Europa Point Lighthouse. Little was known beyond the fact that it belonged to a Spanish national called Rodrigo Guzmán, who'd enjoyed a brief stint with the Spanish police, and had since lived in Madrid surviving on his late parents' modest estate. Neighbours described him as a loner who claimed aristocratic heritage and had established links to the far right in Madrid. The Gibraltar police were still working on the assumption that he was an accomplice of Jardine's, but no one quite understood what his role had been, nor why he had been killed.

Spike was sure that Jessica had suspicions that he knew more than he was prepared to admit. They'd been getting on so well recently, however, that he didn't want to upset her, nor to confirm what he was sure Isola was whispering into her ear. Maybe that was why he hadn't told her the truth about this trip. As far as she knew, he was spending the weekend in Corfu, where Peter was recuperating.

The cabin lights dimmed as the plane began its descent. Beneath the wing, Spike saw the Porto Antico of Genoa come into view, the aquarium jutting into the bay like a petty insult and the green, mountainous coastline of the Gulf of Paradise curving away into the distance.

Chapter Sixty

As the ferry pulled into Portofino harbour, Spike was struck to find the scene so unchanged from his last visit – the same ageing oligarchs squiring the same immaculate women, the same preppy Americans with bored nannies and squabbling progeny trailing behind. He visited the cheapest café in the *piazzetta* and bought a postcard and airmail envelope, stopping in the Gents to splash water on his face. Glimpsing himself in the mirror, he paused. Clean-shaven, the smart new suit he'd bought on Main Street a touch crumpled from the plane, but nicely cut. Cheekbones jutting in his tanned face; tired blue eyes a little more wary than they used to be, perhaps.

Emerging from the café, he set off up the steps to the Hotel Splendido, feeling his heart quicken as he saw a short dark man in a peaked cap standing to attention outside reception. But his nametag was Polish and his Italian heavily accented as he opened the door for Spike to pass.

The same attractive redhead sat at the desk. If she connected the man before her with the dishevelled Casanova of two months earlier, she showed no sign. 'How may I help you, sir?' she asked.

Spike slid his business card across the desk. 'I'm a relative of Enrico's.'

Her blood-red talons moved to her lips. 'I'm so sorry for your loss,' she whispered.

'I know he had a daughter in Mestre. I wanted to send her a card of condolence.'

'Of course, of course.'

'Do you have the address?'

'I don't think so . . . but I know he used to work at our sister hotel in Venice, the Cipriani. I can call them if you like?'

'Thank you.'

She gestured to a low table in the lobby surrounded by deep leather armchairs. 'Perhaps we could offer a drink while you wait.'

'Cappuccino?'

'I'll have one brought over. On the house.'

The table was adorned by the latest fashion and design magazines. Spike cleared a space and took out the postcard. 'I knew your father,' he wrote in Italian. 'He loved you very much. Please accept this on his behalf.' He signed three high-denomination travellers' cheques, then folded them into the envelope with the postcard. The amount matched the fees that Neptune had paid to Galliano & Sanguinetti before Clohessy's death. It might have been blood money, but Spike hoped at least that the girl or her mother would be grateful for the cash.

'Sir?' came a husky voice from the desk.

Spike walked over.

'My colleagues at the Cipriani have found an address in Mestre.'

'I don't suppose you know the girl's name?'

'Giulietta.'

Spike felt his breath catch. He wrote 'Giulietta Sanguinetti' on the envelope and passed it over as the bellboy appeared with a tray.

'Can I order a taxi from here?' Spike asked the receptionist.

'Certainly. Where for?'

'Ruta.'

'Very good, *signore*.'

Spike nodded at the bellboy, then returned to the table and drank his cappuccino until the taxi arrived.

Chapter Sixty-one

Spike stared out of the window of the taxi, increasingly anxious about what he might find in Ruta. How well had he really known Zahra? Could you ever truly know someone else? Suddenly he could see how shocking it must have been for his father to lose his wife in the way he had. Not just the grief, the terrible loss, but the fact of not having seen it coming, of not having known how badly the person you loved was suffering. Would you start to question the rest of your lives together? Whether she ever really loved you at all?

'You want to stop?' the driver called back, catching Spike's eye in the rear-view mirror. 'Take picture?'

They emerged from a dense patch of woodland onto a straight piece of road, a tantalising view of the Mediterranean below.

'No thank you. Just keep going.'

The driver glanced at the map on the passenger seat, then twisted the wheel into another switchback. Rustic villas clung to the mountainside, most of them pastel-pink, facing the sea. They passed a church, a bijou bakery with a few aluminium tables outside, then turned down a narrow track flanked by olive trees. A green wire fence appeared, a swimming pool nestling within, its surface swollen with fallen leaves. Adjoining the fence was a farmhouse, modern window frames set into the ancient stone-work. 'I wait?' the driver asked.

'No, grazie.'

Spike paid up, then hovered in the road as the taxi performed a laborious five-point turn and drove away. He turned and looked at the house. The turquoise shutters were closed on both floors. As Spike approached, his eyes were drawn to a *trompe-l'oeil* emblem above the door, clumsily restored in fresh paint. A single head with two faces, one turned to the future, the other to the past.

Suppressing a powerful urge to walk away, Spike stepped forward and rang the bell.

Chapter Sixty-two

The doorbell echoed through the house. Spike waited, then rang again. He put an ear to the frame. It felt cold to the touch, and he realised that it was made of some kind of reinforced metal painted to resemble wood. As he leant forward to ring again, he heard a soft click from a first-floor window. A clasp being quietly closed behind the shutters.

Spike banged with his fist, then heard movement inside, a creaking of stairs. 'Hello?' he called, and the footsteps fell silent. 'Is anybody there?'

Cicadas sawed from the boles of olive trees. The Mediterranean whispered at the foot of the mountain. Just as Spike was steeling himself to knock again, he heard the long slow scrape of a bolt sliding from its metal casing. His stomach tightened. The door was opening. And there she was.

The first thing that struck him was her scent, not the light citrus fragrance of before, but something spiced, unfamiliar and intoxicating. She'd cut her dark hair short, and it framed her face, which was as lovely as he remembered. But in her cream silk blouse and designer jeans, she no longer looked like the girl he had met in Morocco, but like a chic European, the kind of woman shop assistants would flock to help. Spike realised he was still standing in the doorway, staring. 'May I come in?'

Face unreadable, Zahra held open the door and he followed her into the house. A ceiling light was on, illuminating a large country kitchen with two spotless white sofas positioned around a fireplace crammed with unburnt logs. The restoration had retained a few original features: exposed stone, timber beams, an empty niche above the fireplace which in another house might have held photographs of loved ones.

Zahra retreated to the island in the middle of the kitchen, then she looked at Spike, chin defiant.

'I told you I'd find you,' he said.

'And I . . .' she began in her low voice, then cleared her throat. 'And I told you not to.'

Folded on the table was a pile of cashmere and silk, an expensive-looking leather washbag alongside. Beneath it was a cardboard box, brown packing tape sliced down the middle.

'Are you going somewhere?' Spike said.

'Žigon's been arrested. I have to leave.' She walked towards the dresser, yanked open a drawer and took out some items of make-up, which she brought back to the table.

'You could at least talk to me while you pack,' Spike said. 'You owe me that.'

She threw the make-up into her bag, then walked over to him, arms crossed. In that moment, he caught a glimpse of the proud woman he had known in Tangiers. He had forgotten how tall she was, he thought, and smiled despite himself.

'What do you want me to say, Spike?' she asked. Then she turned away, and in the dull light, he saw that her skin was dusted with a pale powder, small lines scoring the space between her eyes.

He reached out a hand to her shoulder, feeling the sharp jut of the blade. But she started at the touch and he let his hand drop.

'The girl you knew is gone,' she said, and walked back to the table across the uneven stone floor.

Spike saw that the straps of her sandals were encrusted with gems. 'I could help you.'

'That's what they all say,' she laughed as she zipped closed her washbag.

'You could start again. I don't care how long it takes. I don't care what's . . .' He broke off.

'What's happened to me?' she completed, voice thick with sarcasm. 'How *generous* of you, Spike. As long as you can get over it, I guess it must be fine.'

'You know what I meant.'

'You have no idea what's happened to me,' she murmured as she bent down to the cardboard box on the floor. Spike found his eyes following the contours of her haunches, and hated himself for it.

'Where will you go, Zahra?'

'Back to Tangiers. I need to hear my own language for a while.'

It was unbearably hot in the house; he wanted to rip open the shutters, let in some air. He felt his cotton shirt dampening beneath his ridiculous new suit. 'How will you get there?' he asked.

She turned and thrust a burgundy-red passport into his hand, 'République Française' embossed in gold letters on the cover. Her arm was brown and more slender than he remembered, her silver Russian bangles catching below a slim Cartier watch. He opened the passport and saw her unsmiling photograph inside, hair in its new gamine style, small gold pendant resting on the smooth dark skin of her throat. 'Marie-Laure Chamakh,' he read aloud.

She took the passport back, indenting the surface with freshly manicured nails. 'That's right. I finally got a real one. After all this time.'

'Do you need money?'

She scoffed at the question, and he felt the colour heating his cheeks. 'I don't *think* so,' she replied, gesturing at the box by her feet.

Spike peered down. At the base of the box was a stiff leather attaché case. Wedged on either side were two thick piles of cash. On top of each, he made out the golden glow of a two-hundred euro note.

'Žigon told me that if anything happened to him, he would make sure I was taken care of. This was delivered this afternoon.' She lifted out the case by its patent-leather handle. Louis Vuitton, Spike noted, a solid silver clasp on the front, key protruding from the lock.

'Tres chic.'

'You never could speak French, Spike.' He hoped for a hint of a smile, but it was just a statement of fact. Slinging the attaché case onto the table, she walked back to the dresser.

Things have happened to me too, he wanted to say – Come with me, we'll go to the bakery down the road, eat some focaccia, drink cappuccino, I'll tell you a story of two shipwrecks, of base metal turned into coins, of a soldier who tried to kill me on the Rock and a man drowning in the Straits with a rucksack of silver on his chest. But instead he just asked, 'Did you love him?'

Zahra didn't flinch. 'I learned not to hate him. He used to tell me that we were alike. Two survivors. Two resourceful little rats.' Now she did smile, but it was a smile that frightened Spike. 'Žigon said I was the most beautiful thing he had ever owned. Maybe he liked me because I couldn't be broken. Whatever he did, whatever his friends did, I wouldn't cry.'

Spike felt his heart cramp in his chest. He took a step forward but she turned away. 'Please go.'

'Maybe you could come and visit once you get settled in Morocco. Cross the Straits like before.'

'Sure, Spike. It'll be just like before.'

Zahra returned to her packing. Spike watched her, then walked away to the door.

Chapter Sixty-three

The late-morning sun stung Spike's eyes as it reflected off the swimming pool, a film of rotting olive leaves gleaming on the surface, plastic sun loungers browned by twigs and dried rain. A red oleander blossom fell from an overhanging shrub and bobbed in the water, petals facing upwards, waiting to decay. *I was a Flower of the mountain,* Spike thought bitterly, remembering the line from Molly Bloom's plinth. Once through the trees, he looked out at the Mediterranean, sparkling pitilessly away. As he passed the bakery, he saw an old man in worker's overalls sitting at a table, filling in a crossword, biro scoring the thin paper. 'Asterisk betrayal,' Spike said to himself, wondering why one of his father's old clues had come unbidden to his mind. Then he stopped walking. 'Double cross,' he said aloud. 'Double cross . . .'

The old man glanced up as Spike turned and sprinted back up the road, feet pounding the asphalt. The church, the pine trees . . . He saw the wire fence of the swimming pool, the shutters of the farmhouse still closed. He slowed, feeling relief surge through him, followed by a twinge of embarrassment. Then he heard the explosion.

A deep hollow boom, then a tinkling of glass as the window panes shattered and sprayed outwards between the slats of the shutters. Spike lurched forwards, ears ringing, hearing a heavy creak as one of the shutters swung from its hinges and smashed down onto the road. Smoke seeped from beneath the front door, sour with cordite.

Slamming a shoulder to the solid frame, Spike moved to the window, shards of glass crunching beneath his soles. 'Zahra!' he yelled as he hoisted a foot onto the sill.

Inside, he saw that the kitchen table had been thrown onto its side, charred and black, burning banknotes fluttering in the air. He jumped down onto the stone floor, coughing, eyes stinging from the smoke.

'Zahra!' he called again, hearing the desperation in his voice.

Blackened clothing littered the floor. His foot struck something hard: the top of the attaché case, cleanly severed, key still protruding from the clasp. Dangling from the other side was a small metal rivet – the pin of a grenade, Spike realised as he dropped it back onto the ground.

The smoke began to clear, and then he saw her. She must have spotted the grenade as soon as she opened the case, and had some time to run, as she was lying by the far wall next to the fireplace, sheltered by the sofas, which had been blown into a V-shape. 'It's all right,' Spike said as he crouched down beside her. 'It's all right. I'm here.'

Zahra lay with her back to him. As he put a hand to her shoulder to roll her towards him, he felt the muscle slacken beneath the silk material, shards of bone floating loosely in the smashed flesh.

'Zahra?' he said, voice cracking.

He moved his hands to her hips and eased her towards him. She flopped onto her back, eyes open, puzzled, smiling up at him. Her face began to relax, and then he saw the girl he'd known, the way she'd looked while she was sleeping next to him, when he'd watched her in the moonlight, full of disbelief that someone so lovely could be sharing his bed. She coughed, and a bubble of blood burst from her nose.

'You came back,' she whispered.

'Of course,' he said. 'I'll always come back. I can't help it. I love you.'

Tears started to roll down her cheeks. 'I'm sorry, Spike. I'm so sorry.'

'You don't need to be sorry. You don't ever need to be sorry. Do you hear me?'

Her eyes narrowed, teeth biting down on her lower lip. 'I don't deserve you.'

'Don't say that,' Spike whispered back. 'Don't you ever say that again.'

Blood was spilling from her mouth now. She drew in a breath and her body jerked, forehead creased as though concentrating on something difficult. Then her face relaxed, and she exhaled.

'Zahra?'

There was no response.

'*Zahra?*'

He glanced round, hoping that help might have arrived somehow, someone to take over, make things better. When he looked back, her eyes were closed. He leant in to kiss her. His ears were no longer ringing, and drifting in through the broken windows of the farmhouse, he could hear the faint beat of the cicadas and the steady, relentless wash of the Mediterranean.

NOTE ON THE TYPE

The text of this book is set in Linotype Sabon, named after the type founder, Jacques Sabon. It was designed by Jan Tschichold and jointly developed by Linotype, Monotype and Stempel, in response to a need for a typeface to be available in identical form for mechanical hot metal composition and hand composition using foundry type.

Tschichold based his design for Sabon roman on a font engraved by Garamond, and Sabon italic on a font by Granjon. It was first used in 1966 and has proved an enduring modern classic.